FULFILL ME

By
Victoria Blisse

To, Amy!
Enjoy the read.
Victoria Blisse
x

First published worldwide in 2013 by

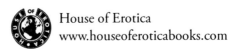 House of Erotica
www.houseoferoticabooks.com

An imprint of Andrews UK Limited
The Hat Factory
Bute Street
Luton, LU1 2EY

Contents

FULFILL ME

Chapter 1

I lick my lips as I run my cursor over his body. I imagine it is my finger tracing over his tight flat stomach, dipping into his belly button, down his muscular thigh and between his legs.

He stares at me. The invitation in his pixelated eyes may be imagined, but it's enough for me! My finger slips down over my stomach, under the slim band across my waist and inside the satin knickers beneath.

An extra illicit thrill courses down my spine to my groin as I look through the window opposite my desk that looks over the workers under my charge.

It's ironic really. I was the best at my job, I never met a computer problem I couldn't fix or a customer I couldn't placate. But now I'm in a separate office, sorting out paperwork and kissing arse. I've been promoted out of my main skills. I don't mind so much, I get to go out to functions (barely disguised management piss ups) and I spend half my day surfing the net, looking for *him*.

My cursor is resting on his chest. Hairless and muscled, it seems to beckon me in. The picture is crystal clear and I can see that his nipples are hard. I can envisage my lips around them, kissing and sucking them into arousal. It's not difficult to imagine his firm skin beneath my moistened lips as they slip lower, over his oh so flat stomach, right down to the edge of those shorts.

My fingers dip inside me and gather some of my slick moisture, then move back to press against my clit. This isn't a time for teasing; it's time for a good, quick orgasm. I do have work to finish today after all. Rubbing firmly in circles I feel the warm arousal spreading through my body, streaking through my limbs. I tense up in anticipation.

My hands are slipping off his shorts now in Dreamland, revealing his large bulge. I sink my lips down over its perfect rounded head, around the hefty width of his shaft and up and down a few strokes. I taste his essence, the salty goodness inspiring me to lick around his tip, seeking out more drips of his juice.

In my office, I lick my lips and take a guilty look around me. No one is looking in through the window that is the only wall separating me from the workforce. Thank God. So I go back to my fantasy, imagining his fingers caught up in my straight honeyed hair, as I lavish all my adoration on his cock. My gaze meeting his, I suck him, my lips wrapping round his dick, pulling him deeper into my mouth, teasing him closer to his orgasm. A loud knock at the door pulls my mind from its fantasy and my fingers from my pussy.

"Enter." I bellow, my scowl intensified by the boiling of my unsatisfied loins.

"S..so..sorry to disturb you." The floor manager walks in looking cowed.

"What do you want, Penny?" I sigh, quickly clicking on my work window, hiding my masturbation material.

"It's just I need you to authorise this, Ms. Cole, so I can get back to the customer today." Penny is a squeaky person. She looks squeaky, sounds squeaky and acts squeaky. I want to pick up a big can of oil to stop her making that damn awful noise. Briefly I scan over the paper handed to me and sign it, confident that Penny has the company's best in mind, she always does. She's such a little submissive corporate angel, whereas I don't give two shits about the company - just the pay packet.

"Here." I pass the forms back and she thanks me, then turns and exits, scampering like a scared animal. I don't know why I have this scary image. Everyone sees me as a complete callous bitch, I'm sure I'm not. I don't fire *that* many employees, it's been days since I last sacked anyone. I just can't be doing with incompetence.

This is probably why I've been boyfriend-less for years too. I was less picky as a teen. Gary was the guy all the girls fancied, so I went for him, and got him - of course. He wasn't hard to snag. My impressively large and pert breasts and willingness to suck his cock kept me his girlfriend all through the last years of high school and college. When I hit university, I fucked, fucked loads in fact, but never dated. I've never dated since and have barely fucked, either; being so centred on my career, moving up the ladder, moving into bigger houses and buying faster, more fancy cars.

It's got nothing to do with the few extra pounds I carry around with me these days, honestly it hasn't. I still get appreciative whistles when I walk past building sites and men stutter down my cleavage when I wear a low cut top. I just have a stomach and abundant hips. I'm sure if someone got me naked it wouldn't be a problem to them. It's just finding that person I want to get naked with.

I sigh, and settle down to work, the erotic spark gone now, just the cooling juices on my thighs to remind me of my nearly orgasm. Poor Nick will have to wait till I get home this evening, then I'll satisfy him. With another sigh, I take one last look at the half naked picture on my screen of Nicholas Casey, the star of *Dobson's Digs* - the best soap opera on God's great Earth.

Chapter 2

I'm not exactly sure when my obsession with Nick Casey began. It wasn't the first time I saw him in my favourite soap - I didn't like him then. His character, Dempster, was stepping in to take over the place of the original Dobson, Donald Dobson, who was tragically stricken from stardom via a tragic collision of his motorcycle and a dirty great big bus. He was chasing after the love of his life, Emerald, who had just confessed her undying love to him, before announcing her engagement to Peter Pret, Donald's sworn enemy.

I'd loved Donald and was distraught that they'd killed him off; however, Dempster's obvious charms soon eased the grief of Donald's passing, and soon after, it was the tall, blond estate agent I tuned in to watch.

But when the obsession started, I don't know. I know it's an obsession, I'm not that loony. I know the amount of sheer lust and desire I have for the character Dempsey, and therefore his real life character, Nick, is not normal. Last month I bought a pair of his boxers on eBay for an obscene amount of money and I sleep with them under my pillow. Part of me knows I should frame them, keep them in pristine condition for that day in the future when they're worth millions, but I can't bear the thought of losing their scent, their softness and that connection to my hero's groin.

I know, I know, I know. I'm obsessed, it's not healthy. I know all that, but I still want him, and now I am working to get him. I've spent long enough dreaming and drooling from afar - now I'm working on getting his pants into my bed, with him inside them.

It's really quite simple when you think about it, which I have, a lot. I've got technical computer knowledge that other thirty year olds gawp at. I know computers better than I know myself and I'm going to seduce my target using my favourite weapon - the Internet.

I partook in a web chat earlier this year. I was so excited, interacting with the object of my lust directly then my plan began to hatch. It wasn't difficult to find out his IP address, or to send over a Trojan horse, disguised in a fan letter with an attached picture of some poor girl's boobies. I didn't send my own in case he recognises them later. I couldn't believe it was all so easy!

I was even more overjoyed when information came flooding in that proved to me that I had in fact gotten hold of his home computer! Now I have a whole pile of information, and the means to bring me into his life.

The phone buzzes and I ignore it, the answer machine clicks in:

"Caitlyn. I know you're in. Are you there? Caitlyn." My mother's exasperated sigh makes me smile. "I know you're there, but no - you'll let your poor mother worry herself sick instead of just having a civil conversation with her."

My mother and I have never held a civil conversation. She's been drunk for most of my life and her maternal instinct didn't kick in until she was left by my father for a younger, better looking model, and my salary became attractive to her "poor" eyes. I avoid her as much as possible, but in the odd moments of weakness, I give in and give her the money she wants.

"I just wondered if your father had given you the news yet. I heard it this morning and it shocked me to the core! He's far too old now for that kind of thing, don't you agree? And she is so, so, so young, younger than you even Caitlyn! And she's pregnant. Pregnant. You've not even got a fella, let alone a baby. I want to be a grandmother you know..."

I zone out my mother's rambling as the shock of what she's just revealed to me sinks in. If it's true, then it's big news - and

Father hasn't bothered informing me of it. Bastard! Jenny is twenty one, a good nine years younger than me and nigh on my step-mother, and apparently is soon to spawn a step brother or sister for me. Right. That's the last bleeding straw. I'll be ignoring him now along with my damn mother. Fuck it, I've got no family at all.

I rub the unruly tear from my eye and settle back with my familiar code and computer information. I can trust that at least - the computer never lies to me. Now then, how to entrap myself some perfection, as Nick *IS* perfect in every way. His hair is shiny like his smile, his eyes sparkle blue like topaz, icy and piercing. His body is toned, his flesh hard and un-yielding, tanned, beckoning me like the soft caramel centre of my favourite chocolate bar. He is my perfect partner. He likes computers, he isn't afraid to admit he's vain, he's into his looks, sensitive and one hell of an actor - just like me.

I know we will get on so well, the sexual chemistry will bubble and boil and he'll be under my spell in a matter of moments, but I have to engineer this so he thinks it's fate, destiny or just a plain old coincidence. I can't email him out of the blue - sirens would blare CRAZY FAN! CRAZY FAN! For that very reason I can't use the phone number I've acquired either.

It comes to me in a flash of light, well, a flash of code, as my sweet spyware does it's job.

We'll do lunch tomorrow, 1pm at Vincentios. Don't be late.

I'm not sure who the message is from as it has no signature and is from a common Hotmail address, but I have a venue and a time and I can be there.

Chapter 3

Red dress - check.

Matching heels and bag - check.

Smutty scarlet lipstick - check.

Beauty radiating make up - check.

I'm ready to face my perfect match.

Vincentios is a regular eatery of mine. I know the owner and I always get a table when I need one; yet today, Tony needs some major persuading.

"I need to be here this afternoon, Tony." I pout and flutter my eyelids, it's corny but it works. "It's to impress someone...a client." I don't feel too guilty, it's only a little white lie.

"Katy, Katy, Katy." Tony exhales as tunefully as he says my name, his Italian lilt prominent. "Not today my sweet, sweet rose. I have a full book. I cannot squeeze you in at that time, it is impossible. Don't. No, don't pull those eyes at me sweetheart. It cannot be done today."

"Oh please, please, Tony. You know I'll pay you well." I lean forward slightly, my breasts hurry forth to impress, my eyes full of the promised payment.

"Sweet, sweet Katy, I cannot."

I drop to my knees before him, right there in the alley (I noticed it was dry before I tried this -wet muddy patched legs are not good for attracting a man) and look up into his face.

"What are you doing?"

I yank down his zip and fish my hand inside his pants, pulling out his slowly responding cock.

"Mama Mia...not here, oh God not here, we'll be seen. Pretty one, my wife may see, oh God, Maria might see. Stand up - put it away!"

I pull on it more, moving my lips to cover its head, to suck and to lick it to arousal. I know this cock well, and it responds to my touch, thickening, hardening and filling me.

I love the power that comes when I'm taking a man's cock in my mouth. The way I can control him with just my lips, bending him to my will.

"OK, OK Katy, you win. I will squeeze you in. Now stop, please stop!"

His sing-song lilt shudders to a standstill as I gobble his length in one movement, my nose buried in his wiry hair, my throat massaging him, my lips sealed tight. One, two, three strokes up and down and he comes. His cock throbs as his liquid drips down my throat.

"Thank you, Tony." I tuck his pecker away then peck him on the cheek. His olive skin is now red with arousal and embarrassment.

"Inside now *Cara Mia* - now," he chides, but I know it is just his way. My blow jobs make him cranky, reminding him it's the only sex he gets. His lined round face cracks a smile as I walk past him. He follows up the rear, tapping me lightly on my arse.

"You are such a naughty girl, Katy," he whispers in my ear. "But my old body likes it. Thank you sweet one."

I see Tony's BJ's as a donation to charity. He gets no action from his old and oh so sour wife, so I suck on him now and then for a few moments and make his day.

"I am sorry I can't get you more central Katy, but we are much, much busy today! White wine, sweet one?"

"Yes please, Tony." I smile, hiding my vexation of being pushed in the darkest back corner by the kitchens. I can be a diva, but right now, I'm in and that's all that really matters. I pull out a compact, and redo my dark ruby lips, then re-powder my face, hiding away all signs of my impromptu display of my best skill.

I've learnt the secret of a good blow job and I use it whenever I can. It's so simple that I am sure most women already know it. Work out what he likes and do it. Big, bellowing men often like quick, shocking deep throating. Shy, sweet, sensitive types need more teasing and stroking. That's what I've found anyway. It's all in their personality if you just look hard enough. It's seen me through university and into a well-paid job. I'm not embarrassed that my mouth has gotten me so far. I don't tell everyone but my blow job skills are something I am proud of.

The only thing my mum taught me that I paid any attention to was that I should use all the feminine wiles afforded to me to get on in life. I was given them, so I might as well use them.

I think it's the only thing my mother has ever said that I've agreed with and I still have feminine wiles, even if occasional self-doubt creeps in and stops me using them like I should. I am usually proud of my figure and I have learnt the tricks to hide my stomach as much as possible from public view. Sometimes, though, I just don't feel like the sex goddess I know I should be. But blowing Tony reminds me I've still got what it takes.

Tony places a glass of his best, chilled white wine in front of me, smiles then walks away quickly, barking an instruction to a young waiter. The restaurant is filling out and there are few tables as yet un-occupied, but still no sign of Nick and it's well past one o'clock now. I sip the sweet, sharp wine from the glass and sigh. How long will I have to wait? Where will he sit? My tummy is aching and I'm not sure how much of it is nerves and how much hunger.

Joey, a miniature of his father puffs over, his cheeks bright red. "Your menu *Signora*." He smiles and turns to go.

"Just bring me the ravioli, Joey." I call and stall him mid-turn. He nods, and races off to another table.

My eyes travel over the other patrons of the restaurant, ever searching out that familiar face. Suddenly, I find it, and my heart beats out of my chest. Nick Casey is sitting less than six feet away from me. There is only one table between us, and it's still empty. I stand up to move over and take it, when Tony leads a tall stick of a man over to it, and seats him there. The pole is talking to Nick and the woman accompanying him. Is it his date?

I look at her again, in her Dolce & Gabbana brown tweed suit and her expensive heels and her very, very old face. That can't be his date, maybe it's his -

"Mother, stop fussing please and sit down."

He sounds as sexy, if not sexier in person. It's bizarre how very real he sounds in life compared to on my telly. I guess the fact he's not funneled through my flat screen speakers accounts for that. Now he's here the plan can commence. Fuck, I've not felt this nervous in years. I think this beats even the time Mum volunteered me to star in a local am dram production. I spent my rehearsals snogging the leading man and not learning my lines and I completely fluffed up on stage and ran home in tears at intermission.

"I never see you!" I hear her deep, once sensual tones and I can hear the similarity to her son's voice. "I miss you darling. Tell Mummy, tell Mummy everything."

"Oh Mum." he sighs. "I just work for, you know, that show you never watch and when I'm not doing that I'm sleeping." He sits back in his chair and as Joey walks past he clicks his fingers. "Menu."

Joey throws menus down onto the table and walks away, muttering under his breath.

"That is not what I've heard, Nicholas. I do read the papers you know, and not that tabloid junk either. I take the times and still read about your high jinks."

"They make it all up, Mum." The stern look on his mother's face must have spoken something to his heart as his expression loosens, his cheeks redden a little and he adds to his sentence. "Well, it's all exaggerated at least. I have to go to some parties and awards, it's part of my job, isn't it Mike."

The pole on the table in front nods then ducks his thin features back behind his menu.

"Here, for you *Cara mia*. Only the best, Enjoy!" Tony slips past me, as well as a man with such a beer belly can, and leaves a plate of steaming ravioli in front of me. I've lost my appetite now but I dip in and take a bite knowing Tony will be slighted if I don't eat even a morsel.

For the moment I can't hear the conversation from Nick's table because Tony is talking excitedly to the tall fellow in front. It sounds like they're both speaking Italian, no wonder Tony is bellowing. If I want to speak to Nick, ideally, I need to make my move now; if I play it right I might get an invite to their table. I'm good with mums - well, those other than my own, anyway.

I'll walk over towards the ladies, which happily is across the other side of the terracotta walled restaurant, so I can wander past his table and then what? I think and take another bite of the tomato covered pasta. Oh, I know - I'll stumble. I'm sure his chivalrous nature will make him leap to my aid.

My plan of action decided, I try to stand, but find my way blocked by Tony, still gesticulating and talking wildly.

"Excuse me Tony." I try to squeeze past him but I'm too afraid of being hit with a flailing elbow to really push forward.

"Tony!" I bark a bit louder, and he looks at me. "Excuse me."

He nods, and moves away from beside the seated beanpole who pushes his chair back. He knocks the leg into my ankle, and shakes me off balance. I fall unceremoniously to my knees.

"Oh, I'm so very sorry," a voice babbles above me, "I'm terribly sorry, here, let me help you." A thin, soft hand grabs around the top of my arm and pulls. I sit back on my heels and fix the bumbling buffoon with all my frustrated anger.

"I can stand up on my own, thank you." I growl, noting the high red on his cheeks, the softness in his dark eyes.

"I'm sorry," he continues to grip the top of my arm, and I try to shake out of his grasp. He lets go and I totter to my feet.

OUCH!

As I rise, my head connects with a serving tray then a pool of thick, tomato based soup slips down my arm and over my dress.

"Fuck!" I cry, stamping my foot in exasperation. Joey, who was holding the tray, is dabbing at me with a tea towel and the horrid man who tripped me is fussing around and making things worse.

"What's going on Mike?" Nick's well known voice breaks into the madness.

"This poor young lady has had a little accident." Mike coughs. "I think I'm to blame actually."

"Wasn't that my soup?" the reedy tones of Nick's mother rise through the barrier of bodies to my ears.

"I think you spilled my mum's soup." Nick says icily to Joey, the waiter, and soon Tony is here, fussing, flapping and apologising. Nick didn't once look towards me, I mean who can blame him? I must look a fright covered in bright red soup. I slip between Tony and his son and head for the door and the sanctuary of my car, all the time cursing that rake of a man, Mike. If it wasn't for him, I'd be with the man of my dreams right now.

Chapter 4

It has taken the rest of the day to wash the soup smell off me. I took the afternoon off work, faking illness. I'll take tomorrow too just so it looks more authentic and less like me just pulling a sicky. It'll give me time to plan my next move too.

I have struggled for hours but I have come up with a silver lining to my tomato raining cloud. I was in the same room with him and I proved my Trojan was doing its trick, bringing me good, truthful information on Nick's whereabouts. Tony rang earlier to apologise profusely and check I was alright. I replied that I was okay apart from the ruined dress and bruised knee caps and he promised me a slap up meal on the house whenever I decide to take it. The optimist in me is saving it for a future date with Nick.

"I cannot sell you this house Sheridan." He looks deep into her eyes, chin lifted, his hand on her arm.

"Why not, Dempsey?" She replies, pouting.

"It's haunted!" His eyes go wide, and her mouth follows suit as she cuddles into his arm.

"Is that why it's so, so cold in here?" He wraps his strong, suited arms around her and stares into her eyes.

"I think so," he whispers and the silence lengthens. His lips slide down, pulled to hers as surely as opposites attract. When their lips meet they press hard, smooshing together as the tongues get busy, and the sound of a hot wet kiss fills the air when suddenly...

"AAAAAARRGH!" A ghastly scream cuts through the kissing and the lights go out, leading into the end credits of the show.

I put down the box of popcorn and sigh. I hate such cliff-hangers, making me wait for twenty four hours till I find out what happens next. I've never missed a one of the five hundred and seventy nine episodes so far and I have every one recorded too - I will watch tonight's back again later. I'll just check the Trojan first.

He's online. I can see he's surfing - oooh naughty boy - for porn! I can see the pages he's visiting and it's fascinating. He likes his women big busted, and I think he has a breast fixation because the video clips all contain tit fucks. Yes, he could fuck my boobs any day. I can feel his thickness sliding up between my round glories, his plentiful juices coating me, making him slip up and down, faster and harder until his cum fountains out and all over my face. Glorious, pity it's just in my imagination though.

He swaps website, and I'm intrigued to see it is a BDSM site. I knew he'd have a kinky side to him, you can see it in his eyes. His viewing material is another surprise; he picks out the movies that show a mistress dominating a male slave.

I've heard that high up, powerful men in stressful jobs often like to have the control taken away from them. I'd take tight hold of Nick's control and I'd ride it away into ecstasy. I have the most beautiful pair of kinky, fuck-me boots. They're black leather and have a cute little spiked heel and lace zigzag across the front, right from the base of my ankle to just below my knee. I picture myself wearing them, a long, teasing cat o' nine tails in my hand. He licks my boots lovingly, I lick his buttocks with my whip, the higher he gets the harder I whip until his tongue is sinking between my nether lips and pleasuring me till I bathe his face in my juices, marking him as mine.

His thirst for porn slaked (I get even more turned on imagining his hand stroking up and down his tool, his essence shooting out as he orgasms), he disappears offline after checking his email for one last time.

Hey Nick,

Is your Mother ok now after this afternoon's madness? She was really upset about her soup wasn't she? I hope that poor girl was ok though, it didn't look like she wanted the soup at all!

Anyway just reminding you of the engagement tomorrow night at Mrs. Harbottle's. I know you don't like her, but the big bosses need her advertising deal. You must make an appearance. I will pick you up at six. Formal wear this time, so pull out the Tux and don't keep me waiting. We have to be over in Parkridge by 7pm, you know how Sheila frowns on lateness.

Regards, Mike.

I blush at the reference to me; I definitely didn't want the damn soup. I still smell slightly of it.

I know that name though, Harbottle, Sheila Harbottle. That's it. She did the advertising campaign last summer. She's a frigid bitch but I got her number, she liked me. Everyone likes me, I make sure that they do. I can be whatever a person wants. I'm malleable like that. The problems only come when they want to learn about the *real* me.

"Hi Sheila, it's Caitlyn Jones here. Hi, yes I'm doing well thanks, how are you? I just saw the latest CatCar advert and I thought of you. I loved it, a stroke of genius. It reminded me that I'd missed your intelligent conversation." I grin widely. "Oh let me check, you know me, busy, busy, busy." I flip through the magazine on the living room table. "Ahh yes, it seems I am actually free tomorrow night. A party at yours? Why, I'd love to. What time? Oh yes, I can make that, no problem. Well I'll see you then Sheila. Thanks once again for the invite."

I dance around in circles then come to a sudden stop.

What am I going to wear?

Chapter 5

What does a girl wear when she wants to impress? An expensive little black dress, of course. I say little but it is a clever designer number that shows plenty of flesh without emphasizing my overabundance of flesh in the stomach area. It's the perfect dress to impress. I arrive at Shelia's house at precisely 6:55 pm. Knocking on the door, I paste on my most charming smile and lean in with great excitement to kiss my host's cheeks, whilst passing over a bottle of expensive plonk. I see her eyes light up when she reads the label and I know I have an ally in my hunt for the heart - okay, the penis will do for a start - of Nick Casey.

"So who else is coming tonight?" I ask as I follow her frumpy black two piece into the hall.

"Oh, I don't know. It's a mixed bag really, friends and clients. Oh, but you might know of one guy, he's big in some soap or other..." Her au fait attitude didn't phase me, I know she knows how big the name she's about to drop is. "Nick, Nick something erm, Casey. That's it."

I squeal like a giddy, yet surprised teen.

"Really? That is so cool Sheila. Wow! I can't believe it. Don't you think he's cute?"

I smile and dig her gently in the ribs with my elbow.

"Well," she giggles, "he is a little tasty, but he's too young for me and of course, there's Mr. Harbottle."

I chuckle with fake amusement, then after a little moment I add. "I hope you've seated me next to him. I'm single, he's single - you could make a match made in Heaven. It'd be in all the papers wouldn't it?"

I know by the blank look that she gives me that this is not the current seating plan, but then the attraction of being famous for matchmaking me with such a big star takes over her brain patterns.

"Of course! Where else would I put you? I am sure you and Nick will have a ball together."

With this she leads me to the front room and into the midst of the other guests, then quickly she scurries away, to change the place settings no doubt. I scan the crowd quickly and nope, Nick isn't amongst the sea of tuxedos. Damn, I wanted to get some pre-dinner flirting in.

As it is, I'm stuck with Mr. and Mrs. Suburbia, who have decided in all their gold and pearl finery to talk to the new girl. I wish they hadn't, Mr. Suburbia spits and Mrs. Suburbia simpers.

"Come in, Nick." I can hear Sheila clearly even though she's down the corridor. She's obviously raising her voice to be heard. "It's a pleasure to meet you, come in, come in."

He looks immaculate in a classic black tuxedo, with a bright slash of red at his neck, making him stand out from the crowd. Talking of which, they all gasp when he enters, then the vultures descend. I hold back. OK, I'm held back by the still simpering Mrs. Suburbia.

However, at least I know I'll have his attention at dinner, and as if on cue, Shelia announces it's time to go through for the food. I head for the door, slipping through the Suburbias' fingers and heading for the top of the queue to be seated. I sit in my place, and am rewarded by seeing Nick's name on the tag next to me. I quickly run my fingers through my loose blonde locks, bite my lips to make sure they're at their plumpest and settle in my chair to make my impression on Nick.

The space beside me stays glaringly empty, as the seats around the large table fill up and I wonder what's holding him back. Then, I see him, walking through the dining room door smiling at Sheila, with his stunning, heart melting smile. I watch him as he nods, smiles and politely laughs at the words his host says and keep my eye on his progress around the table.

17

When I glance to my side, I jump back - someone is sat in Nick's chair. Oh fuck, it's that bloody Mike guy. Is his purpose on this Earth to get between myself and my destiny?

"You're not Nick Casey." I hiss through my smile.

"No, I'm Mike Masters - his PA. I like to sit on his left side, so we've had to swap seats."

"Oh." I am sure my disappointment echoes in my voice, even though I try to keep it buried. Another fucking plan ruined because of Shelia's damn table plan. Oh, and look who's sitting on the other side of me - Mr. and Mrs. Suburbia. There goes my appetite again.

I look up the table to where Sheila is sitting at the head and catch her eye, she shrugs apologetically, but I can see she's not really upset. I fucking well am. Every time I lean in to try and catch Nick's eye, the idiot between us moves his big, brunet head in the way.

I'm not a violent woman but I am starting to have visions of me chopping his head right off with a big bloody carving knife. Ok, I'm going to try the walk past again. The starter was only just served, so nobody is going to be able to pour soup over me this time, so I already have a higher chance of success.

As I walk past the back of his chair, I lift my hand to "accidentally" brush his shoulder. I'm quite shocked when I feel naked flesh, then outraged when I notice I've just brush past Mike's hand, which is now clasping Nick's shoulder. Okay, I *am* going to do some serious damage to that fella if he doesn't bleeding well get out of my way.

The rest of the evening is filled with the inane rambling of Mr. and Mrs. Suburbia and that big head of a personal assistant trying occasionally to make inane conversation.

"So what do you do?" he asked, his eyes twinkling.

"Do? I do lots of things." I reply, trying to keep the ice traces out of my voice, as Mr. Assistant might prove helpful at a later date, though I seriously doubt it.

"Oh, sorry, I mean work. What do you do for a living?" He stutters, looking down at his plate.

"I'm the head of department for customer support at a big computer company, you?"

"Personal Assistant, mostly." He replies. "It's not as glamorous as you'd think." He's preening like I should be impressed, and I'm definitely not.

"I can imagine." The conversation attempt slips away into uncomfortable silence but my heart leaps when Mr. Boring PA pulls his chair away from the table and leaves the way open for me to talk to Nick. Hurrah, at last!

"Hello." I smile over when he glances my way and my heart judders to a standstill when that heavy duty smile is aimed at me. Me, here, in the flesh.

"Hello." he replies, his gaze almost imperceptibly drops to eye up my abundant cleavage, and I flush with the erotic pleasure of it all.

"I'm Caitlyn Jones." I smile, and offer him my fingers for a handshake.

"It's a pleasure to meet you." He replies, turning my fingers over his, then dropping a feather light kiss upon them. "I'm Nick Casey."

My flesh is hyper aroused, the skin on my fingers feel as if it might burn off from the memory of his scorching kiss.

"Yes, I recognise you." I smile. "From something on the television, I'm right aren't I?" he beams proudly, puffing out his buff chest.

"That's right Caitlyn, I appear in *Dobson's Digs* mostly. Do you watch it?"

"Occasionally, when I have time," I reply carefully. "I'm usually rushed off my feet, you must know how it is." I giggle. My cheeks flush. I'm enjoying the weight of his gaze upon me, waiting for the next step in the flirting dance.

"Nick, come on, we have to go! I just had Patrick on the line and he's furious. I double booked you, quick, quick, if we hurry we can save this!" Mike grabs my potential lover by the arm and just about drags him away.

"But I was just..." Nick didn't finish his sentence before he was pulled to the door, just managing a limp wave back at me. I sigh, holding back the barrage of swear words threatening to issue forth. I look longingly to his recently vacated place and I notice the shiny, sleek angles of a mobile phone; Nick's mobile phone. I don't think, I just shoot my hand out, grasp the unit and pull it down under the table, and into the depths of my handbag.

Chapter 6

I excuse myself as early as I can from Sheila's, hurrying out before the boring couple from the suburbs of Hell can try to give me their address and force me to attend one of their garden parties, or something else corny and middle classish.

Back in my flat I'm able to slip the little metallic gift from the gods out of my black bag and caress it in my hands. Lifting it to my nose, I swear I can detect a slight hint of citrus musk, which must be his aftershave.

I can feel the quality as I run my fingers lovingly over and around the slim rectangular block, then I stare into the window to Nick's soul, or at least his social life. It's an expensive phone, I can feel it when stroke the screen. I can't bring myself to snoop too far as yet, I'll leave that for when I get more desperate.

What I'm desperate for won't be satisfied by a phone - or will it? As I slip down the ring tones, I see the vibrate option, press it and feel the powerful shudder of the device in my hand. Biting my lip, I slip the phone between my thighs and press it against my knickers. The shockwaves are delicious, but I pull it away, lifting it to my nose, wondering how he'd react to receive his phone back with my feminine scent on it. Nick would smell my pussy every time he made a call.

I can see it now, his tongue slipping between his lips to furtively lick the metallic case, longing to taste the source of the intoxicating smell.

I slip the vibrating package down my cheek bone and my neck then along the line of my plunging dress, and into my cleavage. I enjoy the feel of it between my breasts as I leave it lodged between my bra and boobs, reaching round me to slip the dress straps down and off my shoulders, then snapping the

21

bra open with one hand whilst rescuing the phone with my other. As the dark bra falls away from my lightly tanned breasts I gently sweep the phone across from one nipple to the other, teasing them to arousal.

My nipples resonate on the same frequency as the phone, and when I can't take it any more I stand up and shrug my way completely out of my dress, then shimmy my lace knickers down to my knees, before sitting back on my creamy suede sofa. I let the phone slide down my stomach and into the warm "v" between my thighs.

I use the long fingers of my right hand to stroke between my engorged, slick lips. I pull them apart, and feel the sticky juices pulling against me as I do. I dip my finger inside, stretching my soft walls a little. My breath catches. I imagine Nick's tongue dipping inside to taste my honey. Slipping the slick finger higher, I circle my clit. In my mind's eye Nicks head is between my thighs, bringing me closer and closer to heaven. I slip his phone between my lips, the solid bulk only contacting a few places at once, so I move it up and down and from side to side, gasping in complete ecstasy when it connects with my clit.

I glide it down, its vibrations too intense and take my clit between my fingers, feeling the vibrations on my buttocks. Squirming in my seat, I manage to move it between my cheeks, and get an illicit thrill from feeling the motion on the rim of my anus, knowing what it is that strokes me there and who will use it next.

My body undulates, my breathing quickens and my flesh flushes. I can feel the ecstasy climbing higher and higher like a rocketing firework, screaming into the air. I pick up the phone and press it between my lips, pressing the corner into my hungering cunt and the image of it being Nick's heavy cock pushes me over the edge. The firework explodes and my body thunders and shudders and shakes until my ears ring with pleasure- rhythmically like a - shit! His phone is ringing

Gasping, I panic. What do I do? What do I do?

My voice of obsessional reason yells at me loudly: "ANSWER IT!"

So I answer it attempting to steady my gasping post-orgasmic breathing at the same time.

"Hello?" I stutter, completely off balance, mentally and physically. I'm almost hanging off the edge of my sofa.

"Who's this?" The familiar male voice replies. I recognise it but my reply formulates itself as if I didn't.

"This is Caitlyn Jones, Who's this?"

"Caitlyn!" He exclaims, "This is Nick, we had dinner together this evening."

I love how he phrases that, it sounds so intimate.

"Oh yes. So this is *your* phone!"

"Yes, yes it is. I must have left it at Sheila's." His voice was animated, like when he was flirting with Doris in episode 378, just before she fell through the rotten floorboards and died impaled on a discarded curtain pole in the cellar.

"I picked it up, thinking it was mine, I have the exact same model." Mental note to self: pick up a mobile on my lunch tomorrow that's exactly like the one covered in my cunt juices that I'm holding to my ear and belongs to the delicious Nick Casey. Ah, I love my life.

"Isn't that a coincidence. I'm glad my phone ended up in such beautiful, I mean capable, hands."

He's flirting. Nick Casey is really flirting with me.

"Aww, you're sweet." I giggle, crossing my legs and becoming more and more aware that I'm naked.

"So, Caitlyn, I really need to get my phone back. When can I meet you to get it?" My mind goes crazy with ideas but none issue forth from my mouth. So, Nick continues, "How about we meet up somewhere after I finish work?"

"Sure," I reply, "that sounds cool, except I've got to go to some guy's leaving do tomorrow night - I can't not go, he's my superior."

"I understand." I can hear the nod of his head reflected in his voice, "Maybe I could crash the party?" he suggests, hesitantly.

"Sure, that'd be cool. Do you know Jimmy's in the high street?"

"Yes, I do believe I do."

"Well, we'll be there from 7 pm." I am nibbling on my lip, afraid to hope that this might be it, this might be my first date with a heart throb. The man I've lusted over from afar.

"I think I can be there for like, seven thirty, eight o'clock ish?"

"That would be perfect, I'll make sure I give you your phone back then, not mine."

He laughs deeply and I giggle like a tipsy teen.

"Well, I'll see you tomorrow night then, bye Caitlyn."

"Bye Nick."

I put the phone down and jump to my feet. "Nick. Nick Casey, I'm going to meet up with him tomorrow. I spoke to him on the phone today!" I dance around, chanting in a sing-song way. "I'm going to seduce him, I'm going to kiss him, I'm going to fuck him and make him mine. Oh yeah."

Chapter 7

"Come in!"

"We're collecting for Stan." It's Penny, dithering and stuttering as usual. "For a gift, for tonight." She stands, shifting her weight from foot to foot, like a nervy penguin. I slip a hand into my purse and pull out a fifty pound note and pass it over. "Why, th-thanks!" Her eyes light up and I feel myself preening in the glow of her envy. I know it's not big and it's not clever but you know, you have to take your ego boosts where you can get them, right?

"Are you going tonight?" She asks, still hesitant.

"I sure am." I smirk back, "And I'm bringing a date along too."

I can see the need to gossip rising in her eyes and I know the moment she leaves my office she'll be off to spread the good word, that the frigid boss is bringing someone to the party. I want every eye on me; I want them all to watch as the biggest star on TV walks in and embraces me, hell the exhibitionist in me would like to feel their eyes on my naked writhing body as I ride his rigid cock-but maybe not on a first date.

Well, not in public anyway.

Nick Casey. It's amazing, every time I think about it, I do have to wonder if it was all a dream, very clichéd I know, and I'm sorry, but I do keep taking his phone from my bag, and weighing it in my hands. My ticket to laying my fantasy.

I spent an age getting ready that night. I bathed, shaved and covered myself in expensive body lotion. I put on my new bra. It pushes up my boobs and offers them on a platter. It will hopefully distract him from the belly beneath. Then there's the knickers, the thin line of matching red nothing that just

25

covers the triangle at the front of my pussy and leaves my arse cheeks bare. I have a pretty fucking good arse and I don't mind admitting it.

I went adventurous and chose a scarlet dress for the occasion. I usually plumb for black, it's so flattering on my curves but the bias cut of this dress and the way it sweeps around my waist, make the most of my big breasts and wide hips. I feel like Jessica Rabbit, only more animated. I feel all eyes on me as I walk into the bar and over to my co-workers. The men are drooling and the girls are bitching. I'm far more dressed up than them. I feel like the odd one out and I fucking love it. I say my hellos, order my drink and settle down at the corner of the table closest to the door. I wait for him and barely pay attention to those around me.

"Where's your date them, Caitlyn?" the voice of Trisha, the office bitch screeches over the hubbub and seems to silence those around us. I shrug, and sip at my wine, acting cool when my insides are burning with frustration. It's gone eight O'clock and he's still not here. I even arrived on time, which is something I'd never usually do, for fear of missing him, but he's not here. He's still not here.

Not only am I being stood up, I'm being stood up in front of all these plebs from work, in this abominably expensive dress, that exposes all my good bits (boobs, legs, the shape of my arse) and is way, way, way too good to be worn in Jimmy's bar, surrounded by bowls of nuts and pints of lager. Bah.

I'm about five minutes away from saying "Fuck him!" and leaving. Yes, I know it's Nick Casey, my idol, my prince, my destiny but Caitlyn does NOT get messed about by anyone and I was starting to feel the sting of my work mate's sniggers.

"I'm so sorry," When I look up Nick is by my table, his hair windswept, his demeanor nowhere near charming but his eyes full of contrition.

"Oh hi," I fake a breezy attitude. "Are you ok?" I rub my hand down his arm from his shoulder, leaning my body in close as I do. I send out a flirt alert to him and a message of ownership to all my fellow workers while they gawk my way.

"Yeah, yeah. Long day of work, some fucking young kid couldn't get his damn lines right." He looks into my eyes, "Excuse my French, but I can't do with wannabes -you know?"

I nod in agreement, reluctantly removing my hand from his strong, muscular arm. He lets out a long sigh. "Anyway, I'm here now, and wow, am I glad I'm here." His gaze runs up and down me, his face a picture of raw lust and I blush in satisfaction. "Want a drink?"

I manage to nod and ask for a white wine, then watch his jean clad arse disappear towards the dark, dense bar. I beam around smugly, but not one person says a word. They all pretend not to be watching me, several follow Nick to the bar and a few bold ones ask for his autograph. I see him shake his head, and push a glass in his hand in my direction, and I feel a rush at knowing I am his first priority.

This is it, this is our fairy tale beginning. I want to remember it, so when *Hiya!* come to do their spread on us, when we're engaged or married and expecting our first child, I can tell them the touching sentimental anecdotes of the night we first met. I can see myself laughing, my cheeks flushed as I confess to the interviewer how I'd been a fan for so many years, joking about my obsession and how I'm more than happy that my desires came to fruition.

"What are you thinking about?" I start from my daydream when Nick places a glass in front of me, and sits down beside me.

"Oh not much, just phasing out a bit. It's been a long day."

"Oh tell me about it," Nick's eyes roll, "I am completely wiped out. It's nice to come for a quiet drink, even with the couple of autograph hunters bothering me at the bar. I get that everywhere though."

"It must get really tiresome." I nod, and see him echoing my movement "I don't know how you put up with the invasion of privacy myself."

He lets out a very dramatic sigh, waving one hand randomly in the air "Oh, it's a bind, it really is. You have to weigh it out though it's the price we pay for stardom. And stardom is pretty damn cool really."

"You enjoy it then?" I ask, sipping the wine, enjoying the slightly muzzy feeling it creates in my head. After all I had finished off a couple before he arrived.

"Oh yes," his hand lands on my knee, just below the red hemline, his famous fingers on my flesh. "There are many perks in my business." he squeezes and smiles. I blush, in sexual arousal more than embarrassment. I can feel the eyes of everyone on me, and I love it. I know all the girls are jealous. I can see it in their eyes.

Now I am with him, I know it is only a matter of simple seduction before he's mine.

"So, before I forget, can I have my phone back?"

"Sure," I reply, thrusting my hand into my little scarlet sequined bag and make a show of pulling out two, identical phones. I've spent the afternoon *roughing* up my brand new one, so it looks as if I've had it for ages. "Let me just check which is which." I swipe my finger over the screen and look at the menu. "That's mine." I put it down on the table then hand the other to Nick.

"You're a star Caitlyn, I'm so glad this landed in your hands, and not with any of those other idiots at Sheila's snore fest. I am so glad Mike made up that excuse to leave, I was about to nod off in the overly arty farty dessert."

"I know," I cry, turning to face him more, my crossed knees knocking against his. "I didn't really want to go, but you've got to schmooze now and then don't you?"

He nods, his mobile still in his hand. "Caitlyn, I hope you don't think me too bold, but would it be possible for me to have your number? I'd like to take you out for dinner to thank you for finding my phone."

"So really, you want my phone number and a date? My you're a greedy thing aren't you?" I prod him playfully in the chest and he looks bashfully down at my finger, then up into my eyes with the full force of his ice storm stare.

"I can't help it Caitlyn, you're the kind of woman a man wants double helpings of."

I giggle, enjoying having the upper hand, knowing my seduction is going to plan. "Oh go on then, let me put my number in your phone, you can put yours in mine if you like, too."

We swap handsets and spend a silent moment punching in numbers.

"So when's good for you?" Nick asks, breaking the silence.

"Any time, baby," I purr, licking my lips. I love the shade of pink that comes to his cheeks as I do so.

"I mean, when would you like to go out to dinner with me?"

"Oh," I exclaim, "let me think. Well I can't do tomorrow night, Sunday night is no good either. How about next week, I've got Monday and Tuesday free I think."

"Monday would be good for me." Nick smiles, "I'll meet you at Vincentios at seven then, ok? Do you know where that is?"

I nod and smile, making a note to go and see Tony, to explain how when I show up not to mention the soup incident. I still cringe to think of it, and I'd die with embarrassment if Nick found out it was me who spoiled his mother's lunch.

"That's great. I look forward to it. I know it's only early," he comments as he looks at his chunky golden watch, "but I really have to go. I have to be on set tomorrow at like, 6 am so I desperately need some sleep."

"Sure, no worries," I smile. "I need an early night myself."

"Can I give you a ride home?" he asks, "I mean, it's the least I can do, really."

"Well, that would be lovely." I smile, pleasantly surprised that he'd offered. I didn't know if he'd properly put out so early. He'll go home with blue balls tonight, though. I do not sleep with any man on a first date, not even Nick Casey, however I am severely tempted to make an exception in his case. I have been dreaming about fucking him for years.

I pick up my coat, and feel Nick's hands helping me into it, like the gentleman he obviously is. We walk outside, I wave to the others as I leave, my hand in the crook of Nick's arm, my face set in a knowing smirk that I know will drive the others crazy. Outside Nick leads me to a sleek grey Porsche Boxster. He leads me to the passenger side door and lets me in, holding the door until I sit down, then he closes it gently behind me. He is a gentleman (or paranoid about his Porsche getting beaten up) and I admire his strong frame as he walks around the front of the car, seating himself beside me.

"Where am I taking you?" I reply with my address and he nods, "Yeah, I know where you mean, it's not far from where I live, actually."

"Oh good. I'm glad you won't be going too far out of your way."

He drives with the confidence and speed of a secret spy. He takes a particularly sharp corner, pretending to overbalance I reach out my hand till it lands on his thigh, and squeeze it, as if I were using it to break my fall.

"Sorry," he croaks. "I get a bit carried away sometimes."

"No problem." I reply, my hand still lying at the top of his thigh. "I'm just a bit of a delicate girly girl sometimes." I squeeze his thigh again, and feel his cock twitch in his pants. I am wet, I want to just pull the lever to lie the chair back and let him take me here and now. Not that he could do that. Driving and fucking at the same time is impossible, even for a big star like Nick.

I lift my hand away, so he can get to the gear stick, I lick my lips, as I think about getting my hands on *his* gear stick that I can see pressing against the crotch of his jeans. When he pulls up outside my flat, I smile over to him as I undo my safety belt. "Thank you so much for the lift, you saved me the trial of finding a taxi on a Friday night."

"It was definitely my pleasure," he replies, leaning over, angled towards me. I tip into the middle myself and land a gentle kiss on his cheek, then I feel his skin move below my lips, and suddenly I'm lip to lip with a sex god. With my sexual fantasy.

My hand presses onto his arm to hold me up and his other hand sweeps down my bare arm giving me goose bumps and setting my spine to trembling. My lips are fused to his, the nerves alight, as if they're melting onto his, hot, liquid kisses which slip into the French, tongues rolling against one another, dueling and caressing.

This isn't just a kiss it is *the* kiss. The most important of an episode, the one where their lips finally meet, fireworks, screaming classical violins and neon lighting all try to take the moment, but the lips have it. The kiss is the main star and everything else fades into the background. When a couple of my motor neurons manage to spark once again, I pull out of the kiss. I know it's important to take control now, to deprive him of me, not to cling or seem too wanting.

I take a staggered breath and unclick my door. "I'll see you Monday then Nick." I manage to squeeze the words out between my raw lips.

"See you then, Caitlyn. Goodbye."

I step out and walk directly to my door, fighting the urge to turn round and watch him drive away. I struggle to walk as the blood is pumping around me so fast, I feel like I've just gotten off a treadmill. Once through the door I strike my fist into the air, and yell, "YESSSSSSSSSSS!"

I startle Old Mr. Connors who was coming home from his night cap. I apologise sheepishly and run up the stairs to the safety of my flat.

I fall onto the sofa, all energy drained, every fibre of me looking back and remembering the last few moments in the car. Closing my eyes I can still feel his lips on me, I can taste him, smell him, feel his hand upon my arm and I know joy. Pure joy at my wish come true.

Chapter 8

The weekend has dragged its heels. I've done nothing but dream of the delights expected on Monday night. I will not resist again and I anticipate indulging in every pleasure of the flesh with Nick after a slow, leisurely romantic meal.

I'm in my element when I'm flirting, I love it. I make love with my words and actions, and I rob a man of his senses then give them him back, one by one, in a delightfully erotic manner.

Work today has been more torturous than usual, I've been coughing and spluttering and sneezing whenever anyone's entered my office all morning, so when I tell Penny I'm going home to rest up a bit, she's quite happy to see the back of me. I know she worries a lot about germs contaminating her workers.

So home alone on a Monday afternoon I pamper myself. I will have the softest, silkiest skin, the most beautiful face and the most alluring dress when I eat with Nick tonight and when I eat Nick tonight because I will, oh yes indeed I will.

I know I have an obsession with cock sucking. Whenever I meet a man, one of the first things I do is think about his dick, and picture myself on my knees in front of him, sucking him till he loses his mind with lust for me. Once a woman sucks a man's cock he is hers in my opinion. She's the one with the power from then on, well at least that's how it is with me. I'm on top even when I'm on my knees.

I arrive at Vincentios late, not very late, but late enough to know Nick is more than likely waiting for me.

"Katy!" Tony smiles widely as he meets me in the entrance.

"Tony, shush," I growl. "For tonight, you don't know me ok? Oh and please don't call me Katy."

Tony looks contrite and nods his head up and down. "Good evening Ma'am." He begins again and I reply.

"I'm Caitlyn Jones. I'm here for dinner with Nicholas Casey."

"Ah, yes Madam, he is here and expecting you. Follow me."

I can see him from the moment we enter the room, he is sitting in a discreet corner, just glancing down at his watch. He is anxiously waiting for me, a very good sign. I ignore the fluttering in my stomach and try to keep my cool head on. I'm going to be in charge tonight, and that includes being in charge of my emotions.

"Hey Nick." I breeze over and Tony pulls out my chair for me to be seated. "I'm sorry I'm late."

"No problem." He smiles broadly, "I'm just glad you've made it. How are you doing?"

"I'm very well, thank you, Monday is finished for another week, so that's always good."

We laugh together, then lapse into a charged silence.

"Where are my manners? Would you like a drink?"

"I would love a white wine, thank you. "I smile and he stops a waiter as he walks past, to order a bottle of something that sounds expensive.

"How was your day?" I ask to keep the conversation flowing.

"Not too bad, I was working with Celia today. We get most things done on a first take. I like that."

My heart is pierced by a stab of jealousy when he mentions the real name of his on screen big squeeze. Has he been doing kissing scenes all day? His lips do look a little sore. I'm just about to make a cute little quip about it when I hear a familiar voice.

"Nick? Nick. Jeez man, what the fuck are you doing here?"

"I might ask the same of you." I scowl at Mike, the PA and all round meddler. He doesn't even respond, just continues to look at Nick.

"What do you mean?" Nick asks, shooting an apologetic look my way.

"You're supposed to be having dinner with the TV execs tonight. I've been trying to call you for the last hour. We need to go now. If we do we might just be able to salvage things."

"Mike, I'm busy here, can't you reschedule?"

Mike goes an impressive shade of raspberry.

"They're your bosses Nick! Some bloody date doesn't trump that."

"Caitlyn." Nick turns to me. "I don't know how this has happened but it seems I need to be elsewhere right now. I'm really, really sorry." I say nothing, just shrug my shoulders and pout. "I should only need to be with them an hour or so," he offers in an attempt to appease me. "Then I could bring some Chinese over to yours. I know it's not the same, but I'd hate the whole evening to be wasted." He's working for it, and I appreciate that he is trying really hard to make things better.

I'd give in right now, but I'm enjoying the look on the wicked PA's face.

"OK, I guess." I shrug and Mike yanks Nick to his feet, dragging him off post haste, leaving me with a bottle of wine and the bill.

"I'll take this home with me Tony," I smile when he shuffles my way looking concerned. "Did that man walk out on you Katy darling? Has he hurt you? If so, you know Tony has connections, Mama made some powerful friends in her day."

"It's ok Tony, I don't want him whacked, thanks. It was just a diary mix up, that's all. He was reluctant to leave me." Not that I believed Tony had that kind of connection at all. His mother was a damn good cook, not a member of the Mafia.

"I do not doubt that, sweet thing." Tony smiles, happy that my honour has not been besmirched. I leave with my bottle of wine and an air of despondency. The drive home includes loud music and me not trying to think too much. That damn assistant of his will be the death of me, I swear it.

Be positive, there could still be a good ending to tonight. Oh yes, when Nick turns up with a Chinese, I'll have slipped into something more comfortable. Slinky red satin I feel, the long nightdress cut up to my thigh. He'll not have an appetite for anything but me. Yes, then I'll get what I want out of this evening for sure.

Nine comes and passes, ten comes and passes and as the clock hand steals up towards eleven I growl out loud in frustration. Where the hell is he? This is taking the damn biscuit. If it wasn't Nick playing me like this, I'd tell him to fuck off right now. But it is Nick, so I will wait up a bit longer and I will ring him tomorrow if he doesn't turn up.

Bah. Damn obsession.

Ding Dong!

At last, the door!

I hurry over, then stop, take a breath, and straighten the hem of my slinky nightdress.

"Well, it's about time, handsome…" I smile my most seductive smile as I open the door. "Mike! What the fuck are you doing here?"

"Watch the language there lady." Mike smiles wryly. "I'm dropping off your dinner, Nick insisted on it."

"Why isn't Nick doing it in person?" I bristle, feeling almost naked in my revealing, sexy nightwear.

"Because he has to be up at six tomorrow to do a scene, and he needs his sleep. We can't have him having bags under his eyes and I suspected he'd not get enough sleep if he were to end up here tonight." The look in his eye causes me to blush.

"You're not his bloody mother," I yell, grabbing the paper takeaway bag from his hands. "It's just because you're threatened by me, well skinny Jim, I'm not going to go away from your precious Nick. You might fancy his arse, but he is as masculine as they come and he's mine. I warn you, if I see you at my door again, I will not be held responsible for my actions. Fuck off!"

I slam the door so hard, the wall reverberates with it. My heart is pumping blood at a dizzying rate in fact it's beating so hard I think it might start travelling round my body on the extra energy.

Who the hell does he think he is? I run to the sofa and grab my phone.

Why do you let that PA push you around? I am very disappointed.

I type out my message on the keys of the phone, then pause a moment, should I add more? In a heartbeat the button is pressed and the sharp message is sent.

He might be a multi-millionaire sex bomb and the only man I've consistently fantasised about for years, but this is a low blow. I throw the filled paper bag into the bin, sigh, and head to my bed. I know I'll not sleep properly but maybe if I read a bit I'll nod off for a little while.

My phone beeps, making me jump. Looking at the screen I see it's a message back.

I'm so sorry, Mike is an arsehole. This night isn't a total failure yet.

I reply, my eyebrows knitted in confusion

What do you mean? Not a failure. You're not here.

A few moments later another message comes through.

Are you sure?

I shake my head, what is this guy on about? Did he have one too many glasses of wine at his executive dinner tonight or what?

I can't C U.

I'm fed up now, I can't be bothered spelling properly.

The beedly boop of the reply comes in almost instantaneously.

But u can c my words right?

Yes.

I reply, getting more confused by the minute.

Right, well open your front door now then.

I walk over to my door and open it a crack, the security chain safely on. I can see a strip of supple chest covered by leather, jeaned legs and trainers, looking up to his face, I smile with glee and slip off the chain, throwing the door open.

"Ha! It's you." I grin and my spread my arms wide. He walks into my embrace, kissing me sweetly but briefly on the lips.

"It's me." He shuts the door with his foot and smiles. What a dazzling sight, his bright white teeth stretched wide.

"You managed to give Mummy the slip then." I chuckle, with a roll of my eyes.

"Mike? Oh God yes, he can be such a killjoy sometimes. I swear he's worse than even *my* mother."

I laugh, and pull him over to the sofa. I take his coat and hang it up then go back to snuggle into his strong body. I know it was rather forward of me but Nick didn't protest.

"I am so sorry about this. I was not happy with him bringing the Chinese up to you, but he can be such a bloody nightmare. I hatched this plan as I drove home." As an afterthought he added, "Did you answer the door to him in this outfit?"

His eyes slip and slide all over the shiny, scarlet satin.

I nod and blush. "Yeah, I did. I was hoping to arouse an appetite for more than Chinese. Not with Mike of course," I fluster, "you. I meant this outfit for you."

"And I love it, you look so sexy, the way the "V's" tease me." He runs a finger down one side of the neckline into my cleavage, then up the other side. "Your flesh is so soft, so edible." His lips drop to kiss my neck, just below my ear. "I could just eat you all up."

He continues down into the centre of my cleavage then back up the other side. His strong body now twists over the top of me, his chest pressing against my bosom, exciting my nipples. His lips find more flesh, on top of my shoulder and they kiss down to my hand, lips skidding in their eagerness to reach my fingers.

Each digit receives a kiss, slipping it into his mouth a little way. The sexual thrill that sends down my body is amazing. Next his lips home in on the other triangle of exposed skin at my thigh. Starting at the tip I feel him dip down and kiss towards my knee. He slips off the sofa to the floor as his lips travel down to my ankle. Lower still, he pecks along my instep tickling me enough to make me giggle. But the tickle is erotic, I can feel it all through me, shooting up into my pussy. He treats each toe as he did my fingers. I'm not a foot girl, but I nigh on orgasm when he takes my big toe between his lips and sucks on it, like it's a little cock. He gives it an expert blow job, his tongue running round and round until I go dizzy with lust.

Moving on to the other foot, he kneels between my thighs, holding my leg straight out to his moth, cradling my thigh like a precious treasure. My fingers dig into the soft material of the couch, just immersed in the sexiness of this moment.

My idol, hero, and all-time favourite object of lust is kneeling at my feet, kissing my toes, worshipping me like a mighty, sexual goddess. I will revel in this moment for months, if not years and decades to come.

His lips slip away from my toes, climbing higher and higher. My calf, then the back of my knee. I never knew it was such an erotic spot? His tongue licking there sends shockwaves through me, bathing my body in naughty goodness.

Higher and higher he climbs. His lips and tongue twirl and tickle, his teeth nip gently as he ripples the material up with his hands. I slip down in my seat, my thighs spreading, urging him onwards to worship at my altar.

His lips stop and I feel the weight of his stare joining the lightness of his tickling breath on my moist slit. His fingers slide up both thighs and delicately stroke my lips apart, spreading me to his view.

"Oh fuck, Caitlyn. Your cunt is a work of art, a delicious dish of haute cuisine." I blush at his sweet, awe filled speech and gasp as his lips finally make contact with my sex. His tongue flicks out, tasting my nectar and I feel it lick out over and over, all round my hot hole and my lips, tasting every last little millimetre of flesh, teasingly avoiding the little bump most burning for attention.

His tongue delves inside me sparking off mini orgasms. I squeeze my internal muscles around his tongue and a deep throated growl is his immediate response. His lips graze my clit as his tongue explores my depths. I move my hips back and forth needing more tension to push me over the brink. I want to splash my sweet feminine juices all over his handsome face.

His tongue pulls out of me, slipping up and over the hilly terrain around its last hidey hole, teasing over the large, aching hill of my clit. His tongue flicks and I make the most obscene sex noises I have ever heard myself issue. I moan, growl and whimper all at the same time as his tongue whips up, down and over my clit, time and time again. Rapid, repetitive and well-timed strokes bring my hips higher as I thrust for my goal. His hands clasp my buttocks, squeezing them with his strong fingers like he wants to squeeze out all the juice inside of me. I release a high pitch wail of a scream. He locks his lips around my clit, slurping in time with the throbbing of my orgasm, sustaining it, fanning it, keeping it going until my body is too weak to endure a moment more's pleasure.

His tongue slips down to my wet hole and laps leisurely at my juices there, slipping up and down and around to reach every last drop of my liquid.

He stands in front of me, my juices glistening all over his face which is etched with raw delight and passion. His fingers fumble with his belt, letting down the zip, he finally pulls away the denim and the cotton beneath and reveals the beauty of his cock.

It's a magical moment viewing the erection I have fantasised about so much. Watching it in all its real glory. I lean forward ready to drop to my knees and take him in my mouth but he pushes me to the side, forcing me to lie down.

"I need to feel that sweet cunt around my cock. I need you, Caitlyn, and I've got protection."

He's got a condom in his hand and I am not going to argue against those beautiful words illustrating the sex object I worship, worshipping my sex. He shucks off his pants and sheaths his cock quickly and confidently.

I spread wide my thighs and invite him in. Kneeling between them he thrusts forward and slides roughly inside of me.

"Oh my God," I scream out in praise of a Lord I barely believe in, but this complete ecstasy, this greatest pleasure brings out the devoutness within me. I worship as I'm worshipped, rubbing my hands up inside his shirt, feeling the ripples of his chest, over his back and down again to his rump. I push him down into me with greater pressure and my hands provoking a growl of frustrated passion from him, "Oh fuck!"

His cock hammering into me makes the sofa shake with the power of his passion. "Oh fuck Caitlyn, Oh fuck."

He's fucking me so fucking good. The word is right for this thrusting action; it's filled with pounding and urgency. Just like my cunt is filled.

"Yes," I cry, another orgasm creeping up on me. I dig my nails into his back, sliding them down hard to his arse, and when my nails bite his sweet, tight buttocks he convulses within me. His pelvis crunches on mine and sparks off my own explosion. My whole body straightens and stretches as pleasure hits. My arms lock, my nails cling to his arse and I arch up against him as he comes.

"Oh my...Caitlyn." Nick flops onto me, and finally my nails leave his flesh. "Yeah." I reply, unable to say a word more. Then after a moment I squeeze out

"Fuck yeah."

He slips between me and the sofa back, wrapping a big arm around me, snuggling me tight to him. I balance on the edge of the seat.

"Ouch." He yelps. I feel his face crumple above mine.

"Are you ok?"

Yeah," he replies, "my buttocks are just a bit sore."

I slip off to the floor and urge him to lie on his stomach. His buttocks look up at me, as do ten bloody nail indentations.

"Oh bugger. I'm so sorry," I gasp," I've broken skin. I've ruined your beautiful buttocks!" I leap to my feet to get cotton wool and water.

"Don't worry." He grins. "I have very thin skin, this kind of thing happens all the time. Well, not the mind blowing sex bit, but the bruises and scratches thing."

"Stay there." I demand when he tries to move. Now I am partly concerned about blood going on my expensive sofa. "Let me bathe them."

I do so, softly and gently, till the blood disappears. "They're only little scratches." I finally say. "I still feel awful."

"Please, don't." he begs, sitting up and cupping my face in his hands. "It felt so good. I've not come like that before, ever." His sincere blue eyes stare into mine, and I know he's telling the truth.

"OK." My breath shudders, my heart thumps faster. I am aroused again. Yep, for Nick Casey I'm *that* easy.

"Don't Caitlyn." He pleads, "Don't look at me like that. I've got to go now, it's gone one and I have to be up in just four hours. I'll come round tomorrow evening. I promise. I want more of this."

"So do I." I grin then his lips descend on me for a firm kiss.

Chapter 9

As you can imagine, I've been no help whatsoever at work today. I have done precisely zip. Well no, I have texted Nick, oh, fifty or more times so far, but I don't think that is the kind of customer service I'm meant to be concentrating on.

It's not like I do anything much anyway, so I don't feel particularly guilty over wasting work time flirting. Flirting is much more fun and far more beneficial to me. I can't wait 'til tonight, I need more of Nick. My obsession has moved to a new level, a new physical level and I am reveling in it. I have Nick Casey. I've felt his cock in my cunt and I've given him his best orgasm *ever*. OK, so he's an actor, but I believed him when he said that, the sincerity in his eyes totally rang true.

He's coming round to mine again tonight, I'm cooking and then we're fucking, his words not mine! So I'm on a promise. I best pick something up from the supermarket on the way home and pass it off as my own. Cooking is not a strong skill of mine, but then the only cooking my mother does is of liver, her liver. Dad is so pathetically bad at anything domestic that he just ordered us takeaway all the time or took us out to dinner. So I've never really been given any lessons in cookery to get good at it.

However the fucking will be all me, I know plenty about that. I've had lots of practice and know I've experienced him once, it can only get better. I know now he gets off on pain, and he wants to worship me. Oh goody, I think Mistress Caitlyn will be given the whip, if not tonight, soon. I do enjoy being the one in control, but not many men I've met have wanted me in control in such an obvious way.

There was the one guy at college, though. We were together for a few weeks, mostly because of this novelty of his. He was totally into the whole S&M thing, the humiliation, the pain, the dominance - everything. I enjoyed flirting with him and his fetish for a while, but then having a willing sex slave bored me, and I set my sights on new meat.

I can't see myself getting bored with Nick Casey though, I mean he's Nick Casey. Who could get bored with him? Not me, I'm sure of that.

"Mmm, Very tasty." Nick leans back and taps his tummy to show he's full.

"I'm glad you enjoyed it." I smile and clear away the plates, he pinches my arse as I lean in to pick up his dish.

"Cheeky," I admonish highlighting it with a girlish giggle.

"I can't help it, you're too much temptation for a hot blooded man you know."

"Really?" I reply. "Whatever do you mean?" I flutter my eyelashes in the classic pose of cute innocence the world over.

"Well," Nick pushes himself up from the chair and comes up behind me. "You are one hot piece of ass, Caitlyn. You're hotter than hot, your sexiness fries our poor male brains and so our cocks take over our thought processes."

He presses into me and his cock digs into my buttocks, showing me he's in charge.

"So, you're under my spell then Mister Casey?"

"Yes Ma'am." He replies, his face held in a serious line whilst his blue eyes dance merrily like waves crashing on a sun silken beach.

"Kneel before me then, slave. Worship my hot arse."

I was quite surprised when he immediately dropped to his knees before me, but I'm not one to miss an opportunity, so I get myself into role.

"Good boy. Now here are your rules for tonight, slave. Number one, my name is Mistress Caitlyn and yours is slave. Number two, you always answer when I ask a question and number three, you do as I say, when I say without question. Is that clear, slave?"

He looks up at me, his face almost solemn. "Yes, Mistress."

"Good. Crawl over into the living room slave, undress and then sit back on your knees in front of the sofa. Wait there. I just have to go and change."

So what would a Mistress wear? I don't have any of the gear except for the whip I kept from my brief fetish affair. I couldn't bear to part with it and had enjoyed many a lover using it on my arse.

I start with the obvious. I pull my hair up into a long ponytail. I look sterner with my hair swept back, I always put my hair up on days when I know I'll be hiring or firing people. It gives me a little boost to be even more ruthless.

I look through my underwear drawer and pull out a black, lacy basque. I remember a very short leather skirt I have hanging in the back of my wardrobe. I look it out and pull it on. It looks great and my outfit is almost complete.

It took me ages to slip into my kinky boots but I knew waiting would make Nick all the more eager to please me. Finally I pick up the soft leather whip. It has a heavy handle, the leather throngs being about five inches long giving it the look of a rather menacing feather duster or mop when hung with the fronds facing down. It makes a beautiful noise, but causes little pain, a good place to start, to see how into this Nick really is.

I stride into the living room and am very pleased to see him, buck jack naked and kneeling on the floor, facing the sofa. I can see his profile, and just above his thigh I can see the uppermost curve of his eager cock, it looks wet and inviting.

I am very impressed by how he doesn't look up at all, not even when I'm standing before him. I grin wickedly.

"Well done Slave, you can look up and view your mistress now. Tell me what you think?"

His gaze lifts up then widens, his jaw slackening as his tongue runs over his lips. His eyes roam from my boots up to my short skirt and my basque encased breasts.

"You look magnificently sexy, Mistress."

"Good answer, slave. I think I'm going to like you, a lot. Now then, what did you say before? Oh yes, you thought I was a hot piece of ass." The Americanised word sounded weird in my high class British accent.

"Well then," I turn round, resting my hands on the sofa back, bending so that my skirt raises and he can see my pussy and arse. "If you love my bottom that much, show me."

As soon as the words were out of my mouth I feel the pressure of his lips on my boot clad legs. He climbs up to my knee and thighs and to my buttocks. He kisses all over them, bathing them with his adoration. He moans and whimpers. I know he's enjoying himself and I bask in his attention.

He pulls my buttocks apart so he can wriggle his tongue up and down the crack, teasing, tickling and arousing me over the strip of my thong. It's amazing how wet I am already.

"You can take off my knickers, slave." I pronounce.

"Yes, Mistress. Thank you, Mistress."

He yanks down the scant material with shaking fingers then he rubs and strokes the rounds of my buttocks as his tongue and lips slip up and down my crack, running boldly over my arsehole. Fuck, this man knows how to please a woman. His lips leave me and he twists around until he's sat on his bottom between my thighs. He reaches up then and plunges his tongue between my soaking wet lips. He seeks out my clit and greedily devours me. I love it. I want to come all over his subservient face but I can't, not yet.

"Stop slave!" I yell.

He stops a second later, and I hear a low whimper, like I'd whipped away a tasty sweet from under his nose.

"Now then, Mistress told you to show me how much you love my bottom, not my cunt, and as much as my cunt appreciates your skilful tongue, you should have waited for permission to give it to me. Now then, stand up."

He stands, his cock still hard, still thrusting out from his crotch, looking redder and more desperate than before.

"Right now bend over here, yeah right over the sofa arm. That's it, make yourself comfortable."

I notice he rests just on the lower part of his tummy, his erect cock will not allow him to rest more naturally on his pubic bone.

I take my whip and I lightly tap his bottom with it, enjoying the way his perfectly tight buttocks clench in anticipation. I lift my arm back, and bring down the throngs on his arse. I love the whizzing thwack that sounds as it travels through the air then strikes his flesh.

"Mistress punishes naughty boys," I emphasise each word with a harder, and yet harder thwack over his buttocks. "Remember that in future."

I can see him rocking forward as I whip him, rubbing his cock against the soft suede of the sofa. So to stop him making a mess of it, I lay down the whip and command him to stand up again.

"OK, another test, boy." I smile and sink to my knees before him. "Mistress loves the taste of cock, and yours looks delicious. I am going to lick and suck till I am satisfied. Now you must not come when I suck, do you hear me? Control yourself, this is about my pleasure not yours."

"Yes Mistress." He gasps as my lips gently place a closed lip kiss on the tip of his penis, my tongue flicking out and catching the soft, sensitive cock head inside. I stick out my tongue and bathe his cock with it, over the head, around it's girth, up and down the pumping vein beneath, he is gasping and panting before I even get his cock into my mouth, and slowly I slip my lips over him, taking him down then pulling back up, once then twice, tantalizingly slow.

I grin. I know he's not going to be able to hold back. This knowledge spurs me on, and I pick up the rhythm, taking more and more of his hard prick into my mouth on each thrust, wiping my tongue over and under it, darting around his flesh as my mouth, and them my throat gobbles his cock. I hear the sounds of him struggling, I feel his balls so tight banging against my chin, and I get a spark of a naughty idea. I continue to bob and I move my hands up the back of his thighs, higher and higher till they rest on his arse. One hand sits and squeezes, whilst a finger from the other probes his crack. Then, timing it perfectly I press against his arsehole as my lips touch his pubic hair, his cock embedded in my throat and I feel him stiffen.

"No!" he cries, and empties his salty load down the back of my throat, the amount increasing as my throat convulses to swallow his load.

"Tut, tut, tut." I shake my head and stand up. "What did I tell you not to do, slave?"

"Come, Mistress."

"And what did you do?"

"I orgasmed down your throat, Mistress."

"And what do naughty boys who can't control themselves get, slave?"

"Punished, Mistress."

"Yes, punished. And little boys who can't hold their loads need to be spanked, Spanked over my knee like the immature boy they are."

I sit on the sofa, and pat my lap. He moves over, eagerly it seems, and drapes himself over my lap. I can feel his cock between his thighs and mine and amazingly it is twitching again, already re-filling with blood. This really must be his fetish.

"Why are you being spanked, slave."

"I was a naughty boy, Mistress." He replies.

"Yes, you were. You wasted that nice, hard cock and Mistress was planning to ride it. I will have to fit you with a cock ring, boy. Then we'll have no unfortunate accidents because you're not man enough to hold your own cum."

I bring my hand down swiftly and harshly. I feel the slap sting the skin of my palm, and his body jumps as the slap connects. Before he can recover I rain down another blow, then another and another, and I'm pleased by the red blush I can see decorating his buttocks.

"Now, boy. When I spank you, I want you to say. "I've been a naughty boy." What do you say?"

"I've been a naughty boy, Mistress."

"Good, make sure you say it after each spank. I slap down hard

"I've been a naughty boy, Mistress." he says, a gasp in his voice, his cock rock hard now, digging between my thighs.

I spank again, harder this time, my hand stinging with the impact.

"I've been a naughty boy, Mistress." Not only is this arousing, his cock rubbing between my thighs, his sweet buttocks quivering under my slap, but it's therapeutic. I feel as if I'm working out the tension of the day on his buttocks. I'm amazed by how hard I am hitting, and how much he's taking. His bottom is red raw now - actually, I think I should stop.

I gently run my fingers over his backside then command him to stand up. I stand next to him.

"Lie down." he stretches out on the sofa on his back, and I lick my lips as I look long and hard at his long and hard cock. I pick up my handbag from beside the sofa and pull out a shiny packet. I bought some new condoms just for the occasion. I take one out and swiftly sheath him. Without much pause, I swing my thighs around him, stabbing myself with his erection. I slip down onto him easily, like a stake through a vampire's heart. He thumps home and I begin to climb up and down him, rocking to and fro as well as up and down, circling my hips now and then, to feel him touching me all around my tight, spasming cunt.

"Yes, yes, yes," I chant as I fuck, "Oh Fuck yes, slave. Mistress adores this cock."

"My cock worships this cunt, Mistress," he replies gripping my hips, pulling me up and slamming me back down onto his hard body so hard that two of the buttons covering my breasts pop open, and I hear him growl in response.

"Rub my clit." I moan, as I work harder and harder on him, sweat pearling on my skin, sticking me to the sexy lace encasing my torso. His hand moves down to between my thighs, his fingers split open my flesh, and his thumb presses against my clit, rubbing round in lazy circles. I pump up and down on his shaft. Fuck, he's good. His cock, feels like it's stretching me everywhere at once. I can feel him throbbing and it makes my whole body ache with need.

The spiralling of his thumb takes me higher and higher, closer and closer to a mind numbing orgasm. I look down, opening my eyes, and our gazes meet. The lust is too much, the contact all we need to make us release, me all over him, him shooting inside of me.

We pant, moan and shudder, riding the giant orgasm that consumes us until we both sag with the excess of pleasure, and I fall down to his sweaty chest.

"How did you know?" he whispers in my ear.

"I just did." I mumble back, kissing his chest lovingly. "I didn't go too far did I?"

"Oh God, no! It was just, so perfect. Fuck, Caitlyn, nobody has ever done that for me before. I've always wanted it though. Fantasised about being submissive."

I smile at him "Mmm, yes, it seems you're pretty damn good at it."

"And you are a brilliant Mistress. Have you done it before?"

"Once, long ago." I reply, "I enjoyed it then, the control is a great turn on for me. It wasn't as good as this though." And honestly, as I remember it, it hadn't been as good as this, but then he hadn't been Nick Casey had he?

"You won't, you know, tell anyone will you?" He asks, twitching, his eyes filled with concern.

"Never!" I exclaim. "I never kiss and tell Nick, ever."

Well, not unless you hurt me. I could do a great deal of damage with all this knowledge and my imagination.

Good." He sighs, his face relaxes visibly. "I thought so." and he rests a kiss on the top of my head.

Chapter 10

"Oh fuck, oh Mistress, oh yes!" His cries reverberate through the room, and I wonder what my neighbours will think. I know for a fact, these walls are not very thick. My lips are teasing his cock again, this time, a leather, studded ring is securely fastened around his cock and balls, keeping him from filling my mouth with cum too quickly.

I can't dilly-dally long, this is a lunchtime fuck and Nick has to be back at the studio in twenty minutes. I love sucking him, he feels so good in my mouth. His cock, tastes sweet and salty, the texture is beautiful, and it responds to my licks and kisses so boldly. I'm just lavishing a few more licks, before impaling myself upon him, when a knock echoes through the flat.

"Ignore it." I hiss and pull open the stud holding his cock in place, releasing the leather strap into my hand. I see him bite his lip, the release of pleasure pushing him close to the edge of climax.

"I know you two are in there, stop fucking about."

I hold in a titter, wondering if he knew just how we were fucking about. I climb onto Nick's cock, even though he waves his hands frantically. I shake my head and slide my cunt onto him. He's mine.

"Are you listening to me? You need to be back at the studio now. Fuck! You can't run off every time a pretty girl catches your eye."

I know I've caught more than his eye. I slowly move up and down his erection, squeezing my internal muscles around him.

"Come on, hurry up! I'm going to stand here till you let me in."

I pump up and down at a leisurely pace. I can see the confusion on Nick's face, his body is responding to the pleasure building in in his balls and along his prick, but his mind struggles with the demands of his stage-mummy.

"Nick," Mike growls, "Come on man, shit, nobody is irreplaceable!"

Nick looks up at me with pure fear in his eyes. I shake my head and scowl then yank myself off his cock and stomp into the bedroom, slamming the door behind me.

Fucker. Damned career, dammed PA. Is he not even allowed an hour for his lunch? I brood in my room, and wait until the door shuts before yelling and screaming and punching my pillow.

"Hi Nick," I ring his home phone, getting the answering machine. "I'm not going to be in tonight, I'll have to work late at the office. Bye."

Ha, take that, fucker. I'm the one in control here, and I'll sit by myself with a TV dinner, rather than let you get away without a big, impressive apology.

"I know you're there." Nick thuds on the door at nine pm and I studiously ignore him.

"Caitlyn, I'm sorry. I feel perfectly awful. Please let me, in. Let me apologise."

I'm not going to let him in that easily, amateur. I'll keep eating the expensive chocolate ice cream straight from the tub.

"Caitlyn. I'm so sorry, I know it was selfish of me, I can be like that sometimes. I'm kinda scared about losing my job, I love it so much and well, Mike scares me."

I suppress a giggle. Scared of Mike? What! He's a streak of piss, as my father would have said. A damn ant wouldn't be afraid of him.

"Mistress," his voice is lower, more strained this time. "I've been naughty. Please punish me. I need your expert correction. Please Mistress, I beg of you."

Right, bastard, if you want punishment, you'll get it.

"Come in!" I open the door and pull him inside.

"Caitlyn I - "

"Mistress to you. Strip and kneel, you know the drill. I'm going to change, I'll be out when I am ready to administer your punishment."

I twirl round and stalk to my bedroom. I know he's watching my bottom sway as I go, noting the rigidness in my back. I wonder if he'll still be in the living room when I walk back in there.

I dress again in my mistress basque and leather skirt. I've got some new spiky heeled shoes that are kinky, sexy and don't take forever to lace as there's no laces. Just shiny black patent leather. I grab up my newly purchased bag of goodies and stride back out to see if he's stayed.

Well, he's got more gumption than I credited him with, he's kneeling, naked, in front of the sofa waiting for me, his head bowed and yes, I can see he's nibbling on his bottom lip. He must be nervous. Good.

"Stand up." He stands in front of me, and I loop the leather, studded cock ring around his slightly excited member and balls. "Now position yourself over the arm of the sofa."

We'll start out with something familiar I think. I place the case in front of him and rummage through it's contents for a while. I pull out the odd item, then replace it. Lube, a ruler, a small pink vibrator, a huge black dildo that almost makes *my* eyes water. I wonder what's going through his mind?

"Ah ha!" I pull out the paddle, it looks just like a little ping pong bat, and I like the way it feels in my hand.

"Mistress is very disappointed in you. When you are with me, slave, I should be your highest priority." I slap down the paddle on his arse, hard. I mean business. "And you didn't do that. You humiliated me instead. I will not stand for that, slave." I slap his bottom again, and again and once more, hard and fast, knowing it stings as the red marks spring up on his butt cheeks. "If you are mine, slave, you are mine and I am your top priority." Another three stinging whacks rain down on his warmed pink cheeks. "And if you can't deal with that, get up now, get dressed and never, ever, ever come back." I walk to the side of him and yank up his head with his hair and look deep into his eyes. "Do you want to leave your Mistress, slave?"

He hesitates for less than a split second and replies. "No, Mistress."

My heart thumps with relieved pleasure. He's addicted to me now, he needs me. What a rush. Nick Casey is my slave after all the time I was enslaved to my obsession. "Right, well I hope you will learn your lesson today, only what I want matters. You hear me, slave? Who matters?"

"Only you, Mistress."

"Good answer," I reply sternly. "Now just you remember that and we'll get along fine."

Dropping the paddle back into the case, I pull out my whip. I love how the strands bang into each other as I flex it and flick in in my hand. I flick it out at his bum, just gently first teasing him, knowing that the soft licks will be getting his cock hard, then I increase the pressure. Each crack is harder than the last till my arm stretches out completely at the top of the arc and I use all my strength to bring down the strands and he screams out in pain.

"Now, if you'd been a good boy this afternoon, and waited till mistress had finished with you, I'd not have to punish you now would I? No, if you'd have been good I'd have played with you tonight, not toyed with you. I'd have taken you over my knee, your hard cock cradled between my thighs and spanked you, the way you love it, but no. No you were naughty, so very, very naughty and now I've got to show you who's in charge here."

I put the whip back, and pull out the little tube of lube. This is brand new territory, and I don't know how he's going to take it, but I am excited as my plan forms in my mind, and I can feel the juices between my thighs, sticky and slippery.

First I stroke his heated bottom. I kneel behind him, and run my fingers over his red cheeks, gently soothing. I add a drop of cool, clear lubrication and rub the unctuous liquid into his arse, as if it's a salve. He moans in gratification. I bet he believes this is the end, that his punishment is over. Ha, he wishes.

I put a drop on my finger and drag it up from the base of his wrinkled, dangling balls, up and up, between his butt cheeks till I reach his puckering anus. I add more lube to my finger, and with little care press it inside him. He flinches for a second but as I see-saw my finger in and out quickly, he moans. I finger fuck him for ages varying the number of digits I use.

As I fuck him, I reach round into the case, and pull out a butt plug, bright blue and bulbous. I run it over his balls as my fingers pull out of his arse. I run the rubber higher and higher till it dips into his hole and I press it in. It's pretty wide compared to my fingers and he shakes his arse trying to push me away but I only press it in harder, feeling the sphincter pop to let it in. He hisses and I slap his arse.

Roughly I sink the toy deeper, now he's moaning and pressing back, wanting more. I leave the plug embedded inside his tiny, tight hole and check out the contents of my bag again. Out of it I bring a leather harness and a long, black vibrating cock. I take my time fitting it together, then I strap it on to me. He can see me, my dick resting over my pubis. I lubricate it, rubbing my hands over and around it, like I'm a man, masturbating. I revel in the nervy look he throws me over his shoulder. I know he wants me, though.

I walk slowly to stand behind him, pull out the plug and throw it to the floor. The fun was about to properly begin. I place my cock between his cheeks. It's not massive in girth, but it's bigger again than the plug and I feel him tensing in anticipation.

"Relax, slave." I command. "I'm going to fuck you now, fuck you for my pleasure. I will press this cock into you and if you tense up it will hurt. If you relax it won't but this cock will end up deep in you whether you relax or not."

I press forward, slowly easing my lubed plastic dick into his widening arsehole. I slip in easier than anticipated, as he seems to relax, which makes me think he's had a cock up his bum before. I hold myself there, my pubis right up against his buttocks.

"Who matters?"

"You, Mistress." he replies, hissing the words between tightened lips.

So I move. Out, then back in, out, then back in. Slowly at first, getting harder and faster as his moans intensify.

"You are mine, slave." I growl and switch on the vibrations. I feel them pressing against my clit as well as buzzing in his bottom. "And I am in charge. I am your Mistress!"

I dig my nails into his hips and I pull myself deeper into him, pressing harder and pulling out faster as the vibrations bring me closer and closer to my pinnacle.

"Who's in charge?" I yell, his reply comes just as I do.

"You are, Mistress."

I spasm and arc my back, my cunt squeezes and throbs, sending ecstasy throughout my body. I pop the cock from his arse and pull him up straight with his hair. I rip off the cock ring.

"You can get dressed and go now, slave, Mistress is satisfied."

His face is a pretty picture, his jaw has dropped, his eyes are wet and opened wide, and glancing down I can see his cock is eager.

"Be here, tomorrow at seven pm sharp. You're taking me to dinner, slave."

I stalk back to my bedroom, grinning all the way.

Chapter 11

Penny knocks hesitantly on my office door.

"Come in." I bark. I'm concentrating on sorting invoices as the team is low today. I'm grumpy because it means I have to actually work.

"There's been a delivery for you," Penny stutters.

"Bring it in then, chop, chop. I'm busy." My gaze doesn't leave the pile of documents I'm analysing. "Do I need to sign at all, Penny?" I look up, and my eyes widen with surprise.

"Erm no, but I think you'll need a big vase. I'll go get the one from the conference room."

The bunch of flowers thrust into my arms, is well, far more than a bunch. A rainforest, a cornucopia, a super-sized bunch of flowers and foliage. I can barely contain it in my hands, and I'm relieved when Penny comes back, carrying a vase that looks like a bucket, half filled with water. She places it on top of my desk on a file then removes the flowers from my hands.

"Thanks Penny," I grace her with a smile, which brings a blush to her cheeks before she scurries back to the floor. As soon as the door is locked, I sweep through the flowers, and find the little card attached at the base.

Thank you for last night, it was a fantasy come true. See you tonight, Mistress. Love, Nick xx

A fantasy come true eh? That means I didn't push him far enough, fuck. Ah well, he was punished, I had a wicked orgasm and all is good. Not to mention the biggest soap star on TV is my bitch. Oh yes, I like it, I like it very much. Sniffing the heady scent of fuscias, lilies, orchids and more I smile, smirk even. I adore being in control, and to be in control of my fantasy lover, the man I've lusted for from afar for years and years is very, very sweet indeed.

As he walks through the opened door, I can see on his face the recognition that we're not going out to dinner. On the way home I bought a new outfit - well, most of me is out of it, so it seems a suitable name for it.

It's all leather straps and studs. The bottom is a soft leather harness, ready to take whatever I want to force up his arse (if I feel that way inclined) and apart from the straps around my thighs and middle, my crotch is totally exposed. The top is beautiful. Leather straps curve over my shoulders, a wider bar slips under my breasts, curving out to a ledge which pushes up my exposed boobs, making them look even more magnificent than in their natural glory. I love the scent of it too, the deep raw tanned scent hits me directly in the loins. I love wearing this kinky little number and I love the look he gives me in it.

To complete my look I have a simple one lash whip in my left hand, and a leather lead and empty spiked collar in the other.

"Strip slave, kneel before me."

He shuts the door and rips at his clothes, his blue eyes almost out on stalks as he takes in my dominant beauty. From the tippy top of my high pony tail to the tippy toe of my gorgeous, spike heeled shoes.

I hear material rip and see a button pop off his shirt as he pulls the white material away from him viciously. His belt is whipped open as he kicks off his shoes, then the tight blue jeans pool to the floor and he hops out of them to awkwardly remove his socks and lastly his tight little briefs.

He's already fully erect, fuck. I love seeing that cock, it's magnificent. He kneels before me and I take a moment to appreciate the sight of him down there on his knees, his blond head bowed, his eyes on my kinky shoes and his hands clasped behind his back.

I press my hand down on his head, then screw a length of his hair in my hand, yanking his head up, forcing his eyes to meet mine.

"I bought you a present boy. Let's try it on for size." I grab the collar and letting go of his hair I slip the wide leather band round his neck, being careful of the slightly rounded spikes sticking out of it. I buckle it up, running my finger between it and his neck, like I'm fitting a collar to a dog.

"Ah, perfect." I pick up the end of the lead and tug on it. "On all fours, slave. I'm taking my pet for a walk." He waddles on hands and knees beside me as I trot around my small living space. "Oh you wiggle your bottom wonderfully," I snap down the whip on it as we walk, loving the snapping noise as it smarts his buttocks. "I will have to take you out on your lead won't I puppy? Oh yes, my pet would love to go to the park with Mistress leading him on his lead. We could play fetch, and you could roll in the grass. Wait for a nice hot day doggy, and we'll do that."

I walk home round for a while longer, every now and then catching his rump with the whip. His knees should be aching by now.

"Sit." I command, and he sits back on his heels. "Good boy. I think my sweet pet deserves a treat. Yes a treat for my lil' good boy!" I ruffle his hair and speak in that coochy voice pet owners so often use. I walk over to the couch and sit down right on the edge. I lean my body back, spreading my thighs wide open.

"Come on, come and lick up your treat, doggy." He crawls over as quickly as he can and his face is forced into my crotch powerfully, almost painfully. His tongue laps, like a thirsty animal at a bowl of cool water. I growl my appreciation as his tongue plunges up and down my cunt, searching out all my favourite little spots of arousal, digging inside of me to flick his tongue over my G-spot, making me leak more fluids and squirm with the intense pleasure. I let him lick and lap and suck and kiss me to a pounding orgasm.

My fingers dig into his head, twisting at his hair and I force more of my crotch into his face as he sucks on my pulsating clit. My body throbs and shakes with the intense force of orgasm.

"OK, Mistress's good boy. For making me come so hard on your sweet tongue you get a prize."

I pass him a condom packet and get down on all fours.

"Come on doggy, fuck me."

It takes him moments to rear up on his sore knees behind my butt and to pull open my buttocks. Swiftly he presses his whole length into me. He rams it in and out of me so fast that I feel my arms crumble beneath the force and I end up with my cheek pressed hard against the laminate floor while he hammers away at my cunt. It takes only a minute of thrusting for him to get to the point of orgasm.

"Fill my cunt." I command, taking pity on him, and well, I've had my pleasure now and I'm hungry. The sooner he finishes, the sooner I eat.

"Thank you Mistress." His orgasmic cry extends the last syllable in an oh so clichéd manner as he erupts inside of me. He crumples back in an exhausted heap. I sit up. "What do you want to order in for dinner? I fancy a curry myself."

I throw a large T-shirt over my dom gear and answer the door to the take away man. He takes plenty of time looking at my legs, and I wonder how he'd might have enjoyed being greeted by me in just what's underneath the t-shirt.

"So how was your day?" I ask Nick as we nibble on popadums and mango chutney.

"So-so." he replies. "I've been waiting for it to be over, so I could come and see you. It was a boring day till I walked in to see you in that outfit. Fuck, that's hot."

I didn't say anything but inside I groaned. Why couldn't he leave the sex alone for five seconds? I'm hungry; I want to enjoy my food with a side order of mundane conversation.

"Thanks for the flowers." I comment, hoping to draw the conversation away from the sexual.

"Oh it's my pleasure, I wanted you to know just how much I..." he stumbles, as if he were going to say something, then thought better of it. "...how much I appreciate what you do for me. I love how you make me feel, how you indulge my fantasy."

If only he knew I wasn't indulging his fantasy, but playing a power game that ups my pleasure eh? Men, always so damn selfish. They always think I do it for them. Do they not hear my orgasms, feel my come gushing over their lips?

"It's my pleasure." I smile, then dig into my madras.

"I thought I'd never find someone to do this for me, you know. I've had to be so careful, especially since joining *Dobson's Digs*. I thought I'd never meet someone who would indulge me like this. You're out of this world Caitlyn."

I blush a little, I always enjoy hearing out and out praise. "Thank you Nick. You're a great little slave to my Mistress."

Oh bugger, back to the sex again!

"I don't ever want to indulge in vanilla sex again, Mistress. I want to be your sex slave forever."

I'm not sure which part of that sentence is the scarier, the forswearing anything but mistress/slave sex or the forever bit. I quite like the forever bit, my whole celeb mag dream could come true, but nothing but power play sex from now to forever more? I can't imagine making a baby doing that kind of thing at all. You want slow, sexy, loving stuff to make your kids, right?

I just mumble into my curry and a silence descends, well semi-silence, the slurping and chomping sounds aside. I finish off, and I fall back into the plushness of the sofa back, bloated and very full. I fall back and the t-shirt lifts up, my bare crotch is laid bare. I notice Nick looking, and since he's still strip jack naked, it's hard to miss the hardening of his cock and I suddenly wish I'd not thrown myself back.

Before I can blink, he's on his knees before me.

"Please use me for your pleasure Mistress. I beg you, please. I need to satisfy you, I must satisfy you."

I'm not at all aroused, and I'm bloated, but I know the quickest way to finish this off. Spreading my thighs I reply.

"Lick Mistress's cunt then slave, give me pleasure."

His lips reach my intimate ones and his tongue begins its expert journey up and down my crack. I'm not particularly amused, but I moan and gasp as appropriate, but when he really sets to town on my clit, I decide I have to do something, my clit is not happy at being ravaged right now.

"Stop!" I yell. "Stand up!"

He stands before me and I drop to my knees before him. "My pleasure is to taste your cock. Fill my mouth slave, Mistress needs to taste the essence of your servitude on her tongue." I'm impressed with how sexy it sounds considering I'm not in the least bit aroused.

Back to the blowjob, I know what I'm doing here to bring him to his completion. I slip my mouth around him, and I mentally switch off. My mouth goes through the motions, no engagement or emotion.

The juices hitting the back of my throat are the indication for me to stop. I stand up and smile, then pull a fake yawn and hope it's as convincing as my blow job.

"Mistress is going to have to sleep now. Goodnight slave."

I peck him on the cheek, and he squeezes me in his arms for a moment, then I walk determinedly to my bedroom, leaving him to see himself out.

Chapter 12

Have you ever gotten something your little heart has craved for? Isn't it great? At first it is anyway, because you've got what you want and that in itself is thrilling. However it's usually not long afterwards that you start to see it's not as brilliant as you thought it would be.

Yeah, Nick is wearing thin. I thought I'd never say that and I question how I can actually think it, but I do, he's boring me. I mean, I don't demand much on the conversation front, but I don't think we've discussed favourite movies, hobbies or colours even. We don't really talk at all.

Well unless you count "Lick Mistress like a good little slave boy," and such as conversation anyway. And that really is the crux of the problem; Mistress is bored of being a mistress. I liked it, I enjoyed it, and I probably could enjoy it again but oh for variation! Oh to just lie back and be surprised, to have him take me just like he wants to take me.

I tried commanding him to do it once, but he only said I must be testing him, that he wanted me to tell him exactly what to do to please me. You see that's the problem. I want him to guess, to find out for himself, to give me things I never knew I wanted.

But no, it's always, "your wish is my command, Mistress." And I'm fed up of it. I thought if I didn't don the Dom outfits he'd just revert to equal partner sex, but no, each time I try it he falls on his knees and into his servant roll.

Fuck, but it's boring.

Yes, I am calling sex with Nick Casey boring. It's good, I mean that man knows how to play my body, but my head and my soul just aren't in it now, the Mistress role has become just that, acting. I've barely orgasmed with him lately; I just fake it, so the Mistress misery can end.

I'm fed up, totally bored and contemplating dumping the bastard. One last go, one last attempt at non-kinky sex, but if he won't take it, that's it. I'm going solo again. It's a pretty midsummer day and as I walk across the grass to where *Dobson's Digs* is doing an outdoor shoot, I enjoy the feel of the hot sun upon my shoulders.

"Where's Nick?" I ask one of the camera men.

"He's over there somewhere, practicing his lines." the gruff middle aged man growls, his eye sweeping over my bare shoulders and down to the sandals showing of my pretty painted toes. I turn away from him and head into the little outcropping of trees he pointed to. I can hear Nick's voice clearly.

"It's me not you." he says, obviously practising a break up scene, "No, Rachel, don't, no. I can't, I mustn't. You're no good for me! Oh fuck, what's the next damn line?"

"Hello works for me." I walk round the tree into his line of vision; he breaks into a smile, then falls to his knees. Oh gees, he's not even said 'hello' yet.

"Get up," I giggle, "someone from the crew could see." But he didn't get up.

"Nick, would you come here and give me a kiss." At my grumbling he topples forward, smacking his face hard into the ground. Bloody drama queen.

"Nick?" I gasp, frustrated. "Stop mucking about and get up."

He lays deathly still, my heart thumps. There's something wrong I'm sure. I go over and prod his shoulder, he's out cold. I move his head to one side and put my palm in front of his mouth. I feel the gentle caress of his exhalation so I'm not as freaked as I was but he's too big for me to move him on my own.

"HELP!" I scream at the top of my lungs. "HELP! HELP! HELP!"

Mike is the first to come dashing over, I look up at him from my position knelt by Nick. "He's still breathing, but he's out cold."

Mike kneels down too and rolls Nick onto his back then pulls out his mobile and dials 999.

"Yes, we need an ambulance quickly. Nick Casey has collapsed on set at Bretton Park. Yes, he's breathing. Yes, his colour is ok. Right, thanks. Bye."

"What did you do to him?" he growls at me.

"Nothing!" I yell back. "I said hello, that's it."

Mike mumbles something under his breath, I don't catch it but from the scowl I can tell it's not complimentary. "I'm going looking for the ambulance. Watch him."

So I watch him. I keep putting my hand on his chest then over his mouth to check his breathing.

"Come on, come on, come on," I mutter. "Where the fuck is the ambulance?"

"Here's the ambulance." Mike pants, just ahead of two men in green; I can see their vehicle coming down the path and onto the hardened grass.

The paramedics check him then carefully put him onto a stretcher.

"I'm going with him." I say as they lift him to the ambulance, at exactly the same time Mike says the same words. I growl at Mike and he growls back, but I climb in after Nick on the stretcher, and Mike follows.

"Is he ok?" I ask when an oxygen mask is placed over his face.

"It looks to me, like he's fainted. Sunstroke probably." The older guy with the gruff Cockney accent answers. "I reckon he'll be fine. They'll check'im over at the hospital though, to be certain."

We just pull into the hospital and Nick begins to moan.

"Thank God!" I exclaim, grasping his hand tighter. "Nick." I whisper.

"Mis - "

I know he's trying to say Mistress, and my heart flutters, "Sh, save your energy, Nick."

He slightly nods and wails a bit more. When we slip through the casualty door, Nick disappears off somewhere and we're told

64

to wait in the waiting room. Mike gives over all his details then we are made to wait.

"Can't I stay with Nick?" I ask tartly but the nurse frowns at me. "Neither of you are blood relations, so you'll have to wait here until the docs are done with him." She stalks off before I can add another word. I sigh and fall back to the hard toxic orange chair. Mike seats himself beside me.

"Sounds like it's just heat exhaustion. The guy I just spoke to said he thinks he'll be discharged really soon."

"Oh. Good." I reply, reluctant to get into a conversation with the enemy. He has, after all, stomped on my relationship with Nick at every turn.

"I told him to wear a damn hat when not filming." Mike grumbles.

"He doesn't like anything to mess up his hair." I reply, not thinking.

"Well wardrobe were there, it's their job to worry about his damn hair."

"Don't you snap at me," I growl, "I'm not the one working him too hard am I?"

"Working him too hard?" He flusters. "No, we're not doing that, we can't get him to bloody well act or work or anything. He just moons around after you all damn day."

"And that's my fault why?" I snap back. "I don't ask him to moon about do I?"

"I don't know what you do, but he always looks knackered." Mike's eyes are wide and raging, I've never seen brown eyes with so much fire in them. I can see orange and red hints as he thrusts his face closer to mine as he argues.

"Well, what am I to do when he comes calling at all hours?"

"Send him home!"

"I've tried to." I sigh. "But he's too damn stubborn."

"I can agree with you there." Mike falls back into his seat, and clasps his hands in front of him. I sit back too.

"I'm sorry." Mike says and he looks genuine.

"What for?" I ask. He should have a whole damn list of things. He's gotten in my way since we first met.

"For always yelling at you." He ducks his head. "It's really nothing personal, I'm sure you're lovely." the last word seems to stick in his throat a little. "But the truth of it is that Nick just isn't performing anymore and I'm worried his job's on the line."

"Really?" I gasp, not realising it was that bad. I'd not been able to watch episodes of *Dawson's Digs* for ages, because more often than not, Nick was around when it was on.

"They're planning to kill him off you know." Mike shakes his head and I catch a hint of his aftershave on the air, very crisp, very clean, very nice.

"No!" I exclaim.

"Yes," he replies, shaking his head. "Which is why I've been trying to get him to concentrate more on the job in hand."

"I might give you a hand there soon then." I shrug. "I think I'm going to have to break up with him."

"Really?" Mike's smile rings through his voice and spreads over his face.

"Yes, really." I sigh. "I can't be his Mistress anymore."

"Erm, pardon?" The red tinge to Mike's cheeks makes him look more human, the dimples almost make him look cute.

"His Mistress. He's a total sub you know. Yeah, and he won't do anything unless I damn well command him to. It was fun for a while you know, but it's getting very boring, not to mention frustrating. Am I asking too much to be surprised now and then?"

He shakes his head, maybe as a no, maybe in disbelief or maybe in an attempt to empty his brain of what he's just heard.

"Well, is it?" I take perverse satisfaction in watching him squirm, but when his eye meets mine, there's an edgy gleam to them.

"Not at all. Surprising sex is the best, anything, however kinky, can get stale if it's all you ever do."

"Tell me about it." I sigh once more.

"Do you want a drink?" Mike asks, getting to his feet.

"Yes please, a gin and tonic if possible. If not a black coffee will have to do."

"I'm pretty certain they don't serve alcohol in hospitals especially not in the middle of the afternoon so I'll get you a coffee."

A dark coffee and two hours later we're escorted through to a separate room where Nick is sitting up on a pile of uncomfortable looking hospital pillows, watching the TV.

"How are you doing?" I ask, perching on the edge of his bed.

"Oh, so-so." he replies weakly.

"When?" I hear Mike explode behind me.

"Ahh, he's told Mike I have to stay in overnight, they're worried I might relapse."

"Well, you're best to be here in that case." I nod. I'll come in and see you later. Now I've really got to go back to work, I was only meant to be out to lunch for an hour."

"Ok, Caitlyn, see you later."

I walk to the door, "Bye Mike," I mumble as I walk past.

"See you," he replies, but by the determined set of his features I know he's thinking of Nick, not me. He strides over to his bed purposefully and I'm glad I've got to get to work. I don't want to hear the telling off Nick's going to get. I might feel too sorry for him and I really need to dump him.

Chapter 13

"See you in fifteen minutes then." I put down the phone and groan. I can't take anymore kinky sex. I just can't. I've done it a couple of times since he came out of hospital last week, out of pity more than anything else, but I just can't do it anymore. I'm going to have to tell him tonight.

Or not, maybe I can show him? Just plain, simple sex. I'm not asking for lovemaking or anything, but something a little more connective would really float my boat right now. I've had enough distance sex in my life; it'd make a nice change to actually feel something as I fuck. I mean emotions, obviously. I feel a lot physically but I need something deeper.

I remember once, I was still young then, I fell for this lovely young lad. He was in the same computer class as me in college and we ended up going out one time. We made love then, yes; it was beautiful, fumbled but beautiful. I'm sure he was a virgin, he was so eager to please me, like putty in my hands. But he responded so deeply in fact I think our souls connected.

I dumped him the next day.

I couldn't bear the pain of loving someone, of giving a person that power over me, to hurt me so much. I didn't want to end up like my parents. I think I broke his heart, well I know I did. He went off the rails, his grade plummeted and he ended up jacking in college before the term was out. I've always felt a little guilt about that but it couldn't have worked out. We were too young. I'm sure I did us a favour in the long run.

I feel I'm going to have to do Nick that same favour tonight but for a different reason altogether.

"I'm not being Mistress tonight." I sigh, sitting on the sofa as Nick plunges to his knees before me.

"Eh?" he looks up, puzzled. "I'm not being Mistress, I can't do it again. I want a change."

"Oh, OK."

I blink, not believing it would be this easy. He gets up off his knees and comes to sit beside me on the sofa. He wraps his arms around me and pulls me close, kissing my lips. I love the feel of a real, deep kiss not initiated by me, not about control, just a sweet, sensual expression of desire.

His hand sneaks under my t-shirt and cups around my bra, his thumb grazing over my nipple, exciting it. I press my body up closer to him, wanting to feel him on my naked skin. I slip my t-shirt over my head and he removes his shirt. I take off my lacy white bra too and we're equally bare chested.

I run my hand over his chest, tweaking his nipples, remembering putting clamps on them, recalling him writhing in pleasure-pain. His mouth wraps around my nipple and my focus changes to that part of me. The heat radiating out from his lips on me, heating my breasts and flesh, bringing my temperature higher and higher.

I feel alive for the first time in God only knows how many fucks. This is uncharted seas. I'm surprised and ready to be spectacularly laid. His hand snakes down, under the waist band of my skirt and into my panties. I lick and nibble at his ear and neck. He pulls back and rips down my skirt then my knickers and they pool around my knees. His fingers slip down over the soft fur of my pubis and one wriggles deeper, between my lips and caresses my clit. His lips are on my chest licking, sucking and butterfly kissing.

My body tingles from tip to toe. I'm moaning in real pleasure this time, not just lying back and thinking of the Nick Casey I once fantasised about. I'm enjoying being here with him in the reality of now.

I hear his belt buckle clink then his hands both go to free him from his pants, leaving my pussy waiting for more. Then

I see his gorgeous, engorged cock and I need him even more. I lean back, swinging my legs up onto the sofa and spreading myself wide for him. He covers his erection with a condom from his pocket and he leans over me, his cock just resting against my cunt as he kisses me fully on the lips once more. I feel like he's resuscitating me, giving me back the full vitality of my sex life again.

I feel him nudging at my entrance, and I spread wider. I need him right now; I need that hard dick buried in me. I need an orgasm on equal footing. He slips into my hungering pussy. I'm totally soaked, more than ready for him.

"Oh yes," I hiss as he rams in to the hilt. I lift my hips and grind my clit against his pubis and moan even louder than he does. Slowly and purposefully he fucks me, extracting every ounce of pleasure from this coupling. My hips rise up to meet him, I am eager for release.

I wrap my arms around his shoulders. This is just what I want, what I've craved for. A fuck with heart behind it. Harder and harder I ride the waves of pleasure and come closer to the brink, my lips pressing up against the curve of his chin and his neck as he strains deeply into me and just as my orgasm arrives, just as I fall over into this new, caring bliss I hear Nick cry out:

"Oh, Mistress!"

And I cease up. His cock pumps his toxic pleasure into me.

"Get off and get out!" I scream struggling from under him.

"What?" He yells, "What's the matter?"

"Get OUT!" I scream once more. "You filthy, fucking pervert."

"What in the hell have I done wrong?" He looks completely confused, his face is creased with worry lines and I'm almost sorry for him.

"Go. I can't do it anymore."

"What?" He still looks bewildered and pulls on his pants

"Nick, when was the last time we just had sex?"

"Erm, a few minutes ago?"

"I thought we were just having sex," I pull my skirt on, then pick up my T-shirt needing to cover up from his gaze, "Then you go and ruin it all at the very last minute."

"All I did was call you Mistress, you've liked it well enough so far."

"No, No I haven't. It was fun at first then it got boring. All we ever did was play Mistress and slave. Yawn, yawn bloody yawn! Didn't you notice I wasn't taken with it anymore?"

He obviously didn't, his face is drawing a very convincing blank.

"Just go. I'm not the kinky Mistress you want."

"But - " he protests.

"Don't." I growl, "Just go, go now."

And he shrugs his shoulders and walks to the door.

"I'll come round after work for my punishment tomorrow." He shuts the door behind him and don't think he hears me screaming at the top of my lungs.

Chapter 14

"Hey Nick."

He walks in the door, that confused look covering his face again.

"Erm, hello." It's like the conversation frightens him.

" I've ordered in a pizza, let's sit round the table and talk this out."

"Erm, talk what out?" He hovers near the door, hesitant to even close it behind him.

"About me breaking up with you." I smile sweetly, holding all my emotions in, playing this for all I'm worth.

"You're breaking up with me?"

"Yes, I am." I reply. "You bore me - no, correction - your sexual obsession bores me."

"But-but - you started it."

"And I'm finishing it. I played along, thinking it was fun for a fuck or two but then it became all the damn time, and I can't live with that predictability."

He does a good impression of a fish, and I just stand there, shaking my head.

"I'm sorry Nick. It's over. Last night was your last chance and you blew it."

"Caitlyn, please. Don't leave it like this, please?"

His gaze begs me to reconsider and I sigh out loud, "Please don't make this any harder than it is already."

"Caitlyn," he walks towards me, taking my hand in his. "Caitlyn, I don't want to lose you. You're the best thing that's ever happened to me."

His eyes are sincere, and a stab of guilt pierces me for a moment.

"Nick, you mean too much to me to stretch this out."

I squeeze his hand and try to release it, but he grasps me tighter.

"Once more, please Caitlyn. Be my Mistress one last time, and then I'll walk out your door and never come back, I promise on my successful career, I swear it."

I nod my head in ascent. I've got to do this for him, he is famous after all.

"You know what to do by now slave, strip and kneel."

I stride into the bedroom and get myself changed for one last performance, my last act for this actor. I'm surprised by how excited I actually feel this time, I'm going to enjoy this, like the big party before you leave everyone you know and go on to a new job or a new house or get married, something big like that.

I slip into the basque and leather skirt, the outfit I've worn most often as Mistress. After tonight, it's going to be thrown away, along with the kinky boots and shoes and whips and cocks. This is my last kinky hurrah.

I pick up my big bag of punishment toys and head back to the living room.

He's on his knees, facing the sofa. His face is lowered, and I swear I can see a tear on his cheek. I shake my head and get on with it. I cannot carry on with this, not even for a big star like Nick.

I put my bag on the sofa, and bring out little, metallic clamps, joined by a simple chain. They look like a garland across his chest once the clamps bite into his nipples. Next is the cock ring, I have to squeeze it round him, digging my nails in his balls a bit to bring down his rampant erection, but now he's trussed up inside he's looking good. To finish it off, I place a leather blindfold over his eyes, making sure the elastic is secured behind his ears.

"Something's missing!" I exclaim, then rummage around in my bag of tricks. "Ah, here it is," I flick open the tube of lube, enjoying the give-away "click" it makes. I grab Nick by the hand

and lead him over to the sofa. I press down on the small of his back and he bends over, offering his buttocks towards me.

I put a little lube on the plug, then press my sticky covered finger into his arse, with little foreplay and a satisfying gasp from between his lips. I finger fuck him for a while then I grab the inch long plug around its widest end and press it into the loosened anal hole before me. A grunt and a hiss later and it's buried in between his sweet, white buttocks. Stage one completed!

Next, I pull out my paddle.

"Enjoy this slave, it's the last time I'll spank this naughty arse."

I swing the paddle and enjoy the satisfying thump against his butt. I'm careful not to hit too high, I don't want to do him any real damage. Three, four slaps and one more for luck, then I swap to the sweet flogger, the many lashes whipping and cracking, leaving lines of red on the bright pink background of his punished flesh.

He's moaning and whelping a bit more than usual, and I wonder if I'm really hitting him that much harder? Then I realise I don't really care. I slap his buttocks with my hand, loving the feel of his heated flesh beneath my fingers.

"Nice and red." I exclaim, "Just right for me to fuck."

What do you want me to do slave?"

"Fuck me, Mistress." the words seem choked.

"LOUDER!" I demand and slap my hand down really hard.

"FUCK ME, MISTRESS!" He yells, and satisfaction fills my loins. I slip into the strap on, then slip into his arse, nicely loosened up by the plug. I don't take him to his orgasm, since I have something special planned for that. First of all, I want my orgasm. I pull the cock from his ass and toss it and the harness to the floor. I pull Nick up by his hair, and pull off the blindfold.

"Ok slave, fucking your sweet arse has gotten me wet and sticky, I want you to clean out my cunt." I press on his shoulders till he falls to his knees. I put one leg up onto the sofa and open myself for him. "Would you like that slave?"

"Yes Mistress." he replies, nodding, "Very much!"

"Eat me, then." I look away dismissively as he crawls forward, the chain between his clamps swaying, his cock, hard and rampant, seeping precum from its tip. His lips touch me, and his tongue buries into my cunt pulling out the juices from my deep personal recesses.

I try hard not to moan or buck back, I keep looking away, wanting to appear totally detached until his tongue laps at my g-spot and I let out a little moan of pleasure. When he sucks repeatedly on my clit I come, quietly. I spasm and my body stiffens, my hands hold his head to my crotch.

"Well, that was ok, I suppose." I shrug. "I'm going to lie down and rest now." I whip off his cock ring, then his nipple clamps.

"If you want to come, you'll have to wank that cock of yours hard, and explode over my breasts." I lie down, popping open the three poppers to expose most of my breasts to his sight. "Then get dressed, and fuck off."

I lie down on the sofa, my legs together, my eyes tightly closed. I can hear his cock slapping in his hand and his harsh, panting breathing as he wanks away at my mid-drift. I open my eyes partially just when he groans loudly and an arc of cum shoots from his tip and drips down into my cleavage.

I keep my eyes closed as he picks up his clothes. He dresses, I can hear his heavy breathing and the odd pull in of breath suggests to me that he wants to say something. He resists temptation, to the last moment, when I feel his lips brushing mine.

"Goodbye Caitlyn, I'll miss you."

I don't look up when the door closes, I just roll over and sob into my hands.

I wake up a few hours later, cold. I run to the bathroom for a shower, rubbing and scrubbing all the last traces of him and his silly fetish off my body. I can't believe I've dumped Nick Casey. I can't believe what I was convinced for so long was the very, utmost best thing for me, turned out to be just the opposite.

I sigh, and hold back tears. I hate tears, so fucking weak. I try not to cry, but my silly female hormones take over at times like this, bah. I dumped him so why am I so sad?

"The camera!" I yell, rushing out of the shower and into a towel. Quickly I dry off, then run into my bedroom, flinging on my pyjamas then running into my front room. Just on top of my computer is a small camera. I never use it really; it just came as part of my PC package. However, this evening I have used it.

Slipping into my comfortable swivel chair, I switch on the computer monitor, click on the software and watch the video recording of the sex acts that happened before. Carefully I capture some images, one of Nick in nipple clamps and cock ring, his face uncovered. A few of his reddened arse, a few of him licking my cunt, then a beautiful one of his cum splashing over my chest. In each photo, only my body shows, never my face.

I take one of them, and compose a teasing email to send to the tabloids. I hover over the send for a moment, but then I click. I've got to think of what is best for me and I need to come out of this with something positive, a big money deal would just about do the trick.

One hour later I have a reply, and the next day, I have a good amount more money in my bank account and the highest bidder has a front page spread.

And I have to say, my thighs look particularly good in the front page picture, even if it's a little grainy and my stomach is hidden from view by his big head.

Chapter 15

God bless you Chocolate fudge brownie Ice cream. You are a dream come true for a woman whose dream has been well and truly shattered at her very own hands.

Why couldn't I be his Mistress? Why not. I mean, sex isn't everything in a relationship is it? But then what was in Nick and I's relationship that wasn't sex? Exactly. That's why I had to end it, end the sweet, sweet dream of a life in a mansion, with regular spots in Hiya! magazine. Woe is me.

However, I have ice cream in my hand and Jerry Maguire on the TV, so I'll heal. I always do. It's not like I was in love with him. Ok, so I had been obsessed with him, you can't deny that, and maybe I'd built him up to be something more than human in my mind.

I can't even remember how it felt to be so taken with him, to want him so much. Though I've had him now, and found him not that entertaining. Fuck, I wish I could have put up with it, a few years, a messy divorce and I'd be set up for life.

But no, I always said I'd never go the way of my mother. Never. However she did sell her story to a sleazy rag that time, but this is totally different. I'm not pregnant for a start.

A knock startled me from my thoughts. The door? Who could it be? I open it, leaving the chain on.

"Who is it?"

"Mike." He growls.

"Oh. What do you want?"

"I think you know exactly what I want!"

"That would be the whore house round the corner."

I try and shut the door, but he puts his foot in the way.

"Ha, bloody ha. Just let me in."

"Why should I?" I snap.

"Because if you don't I'm going to make a right scene on your doorstep."

I wish I could say I don't care, but I do, so I let the chain drop and shuffle back to the living room.

"What the hell were you thinking?" Mike strides into the room, his crisp citrus scent mixed with the subtle taint of early autumn rain. I walk to the sofa, pick up the tub of ice cream and continue to watch my film.

"I said, what do you think you were doing?" he's standing directly in front of me now. I'm staring right at the crotch of his black jeans.

I look up, shrug, and look back at the TV. He vents his frustration in a low pitched growl then sits down on the sofa next to me.

"Why did you tell the papers all that about Nick?"

"Because." He's not going to get an ounce of information, retribution or whatever from me.

"Why did you make up all that bollocks?"

"I didn't make it up. Everything I told them was one hundred percenttrue."

"Oh, come of it. You don't think I'll swallow that."

"Did you not see the pictures?" I reply, getting a bit pissed off by his presence, the fact I'm in my oldest, comfiest pyjamas not helping my mood. I feel frumpy and vulnerable.

"You can fake pictures."

"Right." I slam down the spoon on the table, followed by my rapidly melting ice cream and stride over to the computer.

I switch on, find the video and start it running.

"Watch this. It's the video I took the screen caps from."

I stalk back to the sofa, and try desperately to listen to Jerry Maguire and not the yells and whelps of Nick Casey.

"I don't want to watch anymore." after five minutes, he clicks off the computer. "Ok so it's true, but I still don't know why you took it to the papers."

"Oh use your damn imagination, if you have one." I snap, thoroughly sick of this masculine invasion of my very feminine grieving period.

"Money, revenge, pettiness."

"Well two out of three isn't bad. Now you know, do you think there's a chance of you fucking off, so I can watch my movie in peace?"

"You are such a lady." He sneers at me. "But no, I'm not going 'til you realise what you've done. You've ruined his career. He's been written out of *Dobson's Digs*, killed off completely. He's been embarrassed in public, his mum has disowned him and on top of all that I've been sacked too. An out of work actor doesn't need a damn PA!"

"Diddums." I coo sarcastically. "I feel so bad, honestly I do. Now will you fuck off? What's done is done. I can't change it."

"You have no conscience do you?"

"How do you know? You don't know me. You don't know what I'm thinking or feeling, you don't have a fucking clue what I've given up, what I've settled for."

This man gets my back up, he really does.

"I don't care," he snaps. "I just wanted you to realise the consequences of your bratty actions."

"Well gee thanks, that's so helpful. Now will you fuck off?"

"Yes!" he snaps "I will!" and off he storms out of my door.

I lock and bolt it after him, a tear sliding down my cheek. I know what I did and I'm not proud of it. I didn't mean for it to put Nick out of a job, I wanted it to boost his ratings. No, it seems I sold him down the river for my retirement fund. Fuck it, there's nothing I can do now. Nick will bounce back and I don't give a shit about dead-end Mike and his damned annoying attitude.

I'll get on with my life and they can sort out their own. It's not my responsibility. I'm only responsible for me and my happiness, and right now my happiness needs ice cream, lots and lots of ice cream.

I can't concentrate on Jerry any more though, I keep getting images of a poor dejected Nick, and my hand keeps hovering over the mobile. Should I ring? I should apologise at least. But what if he yells at me, or worse comes round here? I couldn't face him now, I'd fall apart.

Email! I'll send him an Email! Yes, an Email will do the trick.

Dear Nick,

I know you probably don't want to hear from me ever again, I can totally understand that, however I must apologise for what I've done.

It was a silly, childish knee jerk reaction and I really didn't think it'd hold such serious repercussions for you. I apologise from the bottom of my heart, I never wanted to really hurt you. I did want revenge, I did want to make something from our relationship, and I have really beaten myself up for my selfish attitude.

I can't say sorry enough and I know I can't make it better. I just have to try to make you realise I didn't mean it.

Take care,
Caitlyn xxx

I click send, and breathe a sigh of relief. It's gone now, and even if he never reads it or replies, I know my apology has been said, it's all I can do really. I shut down the computer and my phone rings. I pick it up.

"Hey Caitlyn, it's Daddy here."

"Oh, hey Dad." I sigh. Only my father would ring at 11:30pm. "What's up?"

"Nothing, nothing," he replies hastily, "Does something have to be up for me to call you?"

"Yes, it usually does. How are you?"

"I'm doing good. How's my baby girl?"

I hate it when he pulls out the old pet names for me. It's a long time since I was his baby girl. I grew out of being impressed by affectionate names twenty years ago.

"I'm good Dad. Just about to go to bed." Hint hint, father dearest.

"Oh right, is it late? Yeah, I suppose it is. Anyway, I was ringing to tell you Jenny and I are getting married."

"I know." I sigh, "Nice of you to finally tell me."

"How did you find out?" My father snaps. "Well, it doesn't matter, all that matters is you being there this Saturday."

This Saturday? Well thanks for the notice!

I pause and he asks, obviously uncomfortable with the conversation.

"Will you be there? Jenny and I have some other news to announce too."

So the bitch is preggers. Oh great! This will be such a fun way to get over Nick, but then again maybe it could be. Weddings are always good for sex...

"Alright Dad, I'll be there."

"Oh good," he sighs in relief. "See you Saturday at St Martins, eleven am. Ok? I'm glad you're coming, Daddy misses his special girl."

"Yeah, bye Dad."

I put the phone down before he gets even creepier. Daddy's special girl my arse, he barely thinks about me. He's never been very paternal, leaving me with my drunk mother for 90% of my crappy childhood. He was too busy making his millions and fucking young girls to bother with his own daughter.

I wonder why he's so desperate to include me now? Probably doesn't want any bad publicity in the paper, he's got to play happy families for the big occasion.

Chapter 16

"Katy! It is so good to see you; do you need a table for two?" Tony beams, wrapping me in a hug and kissing each cheek tenderly.

"Not tonight Tony, I'm flying solo right now." Such an early reminder of my singledom, I knew I shouldn't have done this, I was just so sick of staring at the four same walls all the damn time.

"That is criminal, *Ma Bella*! But all is not lost. My son, Joseph is just about to finish his shift, I am sure he would love to join you this evening."

"That would be delightful." I smile at Tony; Joey is very sexy with his sweet Italian looks and good fashion taste. He's young, fit and eager no doubt. Yes, I need to get back in the game, after almost a month of celibacy. I need something carnal to satisfy me.

"Ok, Katy. Sit, sit. I shall bring him over now." Tony fusses off in the direction of the kitchens and I sit on the red plush chair and stare at the window, black as ice on a country road now that the nights are drawing in, I miss the long days of summer, but the leaves changing colour and the longer nights seems to fit in with my current melancholy frame of mind.

"Caitlyn. My father believes you're in need of an escort for tonight." Joey appears, dressed immaculately in black dress pants and a beautiful white shirt that shows of his dark features to a tee.

"I do Joe, but I'm not going to pay you for it."

"Of course not *cara mia*!" He throws his hands in the air dramatically "Just being with a woman of your beauty is reward enough." I grin widely.

"You're a smooth one Joey. I like smooth men, they feel so good against my skin."

His hard brown eyes soften with a sparkle of lust. "And your skin looks like it would feel wonderful against my lips." He picks my hand up from the table, and brushes the knuckles with his lips. Oh yes, this is going to be a good night.

The waiter brings over the wine and Joey orders for us both. I find it's always prudent to go with what a waiter recommends as he sees the food as it's prepared and knows which ingredients are the freshest and best on this day. We eat, chat and flirt. I love flirting, it is like fire in my blood, it's the life of me. I feel on top of things in a way I've not been in a long time. I love the feeling of control as we play the attraction game.

Joey is an open book; he's easily read and easily picked up. After our meal, as we sip coffee he casually suggests I go back to his for a night cap.

"That sounds lovely." I reply, "Thank you."

"It's my pleasure." he holds open my coat and when I slip into it he runs his hand up and down my arms to smooth out the material and stir my blood. He kisses me gently on the cheek then leads me out to the taxi waiting there for us.

He lets me in first then slips in beside me telling the cabby the details of his student digs.

"The guys are all out tonight. They'll not be back to the early hours, so we can have our nightcap in peace." His hand wraps around my shoulders and I lean into his arm, my body alive with tingles and sexual shocks.

"Lovely. Though if your friends are as handsome as you, I think I could take them all on." I must have drunk a little too much wine; I always get a little forward with excess alcohol in my bloodstream.

"Well, we'll see what happens." Joey winks and nibbles my neck, hitting a favourite erogenous zone of mine. I brush down his chest with my fingers splayed, slipping briefly over his stirring crotch and landing squarely on his thigh.

He moans and slides a hand inside my coat. At the same time he gets inside my low cut top to clutch at breasts. Joey obviously likes them because with every squeeze he moans. He presses his mouth to mine and kisses me deeply.

Europeans kiss so thoroughly and with great art. My lips, teeth and even gums feel turned on. They're enveloped in a kiss that keeps so much of my concentration above the neck even though a strong rough hand is skillfully manipulating my breast.

"We're here." his lips disengage from mine, and we exit the cab. He passes the driver a twenty. He waves away the change and we walk through the sharp night air to the looming block of flats before us. "We're best taking the stairs." He smiles, "It's only a few floors up and I don't trust the lift."

I shrug, "Lead the way." Joey slips his arm around my waist and we begin the ascent. The higher up the stairs we go, the lower his hand sits. On my hip, in the small of my back, on the curve of my bottom then his palm is cupping and squeezing my buttock as we climb.

"Here we are." He pinches my arse, cheekily and fumbles in his pocket, pulling out his key to open the locked door. I follow him into a dark room. A lamp comes on and I'm surprised by the cleanliness but then I realise, the guys are out on the pull, they'll be hoping to bring girls home tonight, and a dirty room is not going to get anyone laid.

I slam the door shut behind me and suddenly I'm in Joey's arms. I'm swept away by the ferocity of his embrace, his lips seek out mine. He throws my coat from my shoulders to the floor and walks backwards, leading me somewhere. I let myself be led, running my hands up under his shirt, feeling his strong back and hearing him groan when my cool fingers hit his warm flesh.

Moving around to the front I struggle with the buttons on his shirt, our lips still linked, one of his hands in my hair, the other cupping the side of my breast. Finally, I free all the buttons and push the material away to expose his body. I slip my lips to his cheek, down his neck, lower to his chest. He growls and moans, and I feel the shock of his body hitting up against something hard. I use the cease in momentum to press my body against him; I grind my pelvis against him then nibble on his shoulder. His chest, nipples and stomach feel the skim of lips while I pull at his belt, and loosen his trousers.

As I do, the solid object clicks and swings open and I stagger into another room, giggling when I'm set off balance. He catches me just below my shoulder, spinning me round again till I'm dizzy and giggling and falling. Thankfully I land on the soft, masculine smelling duvet covering Joey's bed and his body crushes down on me.

He's removed his trousers so I am clothed, and he is naked. He begins to work on changing that, slipping up the skirt at my waist and stripping away my knickers. He strokes and teases my thighs as his lips search out the flesh of my chest, dipping into my cleavage. I pull up my top and pull it out of the way. He wraps his arms around me and pops open my bra so he can get his lips around my nipple. Joey devours my tits and his fingers seek out the wet juices on my thighs and what lies between them.

My body is attacked from all angles and the pleasures are melting and melding into each other to make me feel like a hot cup of freshly made coffee, yearning to be drunk. His body shifts so his head faces my toes and his toes disappear above my head. My fingers seek out the contours of his back and down to his buttocks and thighs. Under him I find his cock. It's hefty, eager and I want to taste it but first I experience it with my fingers.

He nuzzles between my thighs and seeks out my clit. I feverishly caress him, echoing the strokes of his tongue. I lick and nibble at the flesh I can reach then he grasps my buttocks and turns me to the side, delving deeper between my thighs. He exposes his erection to me and I can finally wrap my lips around it. He tastes divine. Sweet and tangy and oh so very masculine, I cannot get enough of his salted caramel taste. I drive my mouth to the base of him then pull up to the tip. I gently grasp his bollocks as my lips feel around the flesh of his cock.

He moans and writhes. I know my mouth is becoming too much for him. He lifts away from my muff and he forces himself away from me. I mewl for him, needing that taste, but once he turns around he hushes me with his mouth and the melding of our tastes. The fusion of which is fantastic. It's like apple pie and custard, two tastes that are meant to be enjoyed together.

He reaches up to the bedside and grabs a condom. I nod as he waves it at me. An unspoken signal of consent. He drops back and while his lips thoroughly entertain mine I can feel him slipping the condom on. Wow, he must be well practiced at it. He settles between my thighs and I open eagerly for him. His tongue thrusts into my mouth at the same time his cock enters my cunt in a fluid motion, filling me and stretching me, making me scream into his mouth. He nibbles on my bottom lip and it makes my clit twitch erotically.

I gasp as he fucks me and chases his lips with mine. I feel him swell inside me and I squeeze my internal muscles, causing a flood of pleasure through me, and hopefully through him too. As I contract, the touch of his flesh against my clit sets off an orgasm which ripples and grows over and over until he thrusts one last time, biting into the soft flesh of my throat and flooding me with his come. I scream and juices roll down my thighs, squeezed out by the contractions of my pleasure.

My shoulders slump and I hear the sounds of applause, and I wonder if I've perforated my eardrum or something. Looking up I see another two men at the door, clapping and whistling. They obviously enjoyed the show.

"Thank you, thank you," I grin. "Give me five minutes, and I'll show you my encore."

Whoops of pleasure issue from their soft, young Italian lips, including Joey's.

"I like having an audience." I giggle, sitting up so the lads in the doorway can see my boobs. Joey leans back on his elbows grinning like the preverbal cat.

"Give them a proper show," he urges, elbowing me just below my ribs.

"Yeah, give us a proper show!" They roar as if the sight of me fucking wasn't a show enough for them. I shrug; I'm still young, still sexy and still horny-so why not? I might be older than all three guys but that makes the thrill all the sexier.

I jump off the bed, my skirt slithering back down over my limbs. I kink my hips from side to side and turn around, running my hands down over my breasts to my hips. More roars and whoops are emitted and I hook my thumbs under my waistband and start to shimmy down my skirt. I turn round slowly and shimmy, winking broadly, and grinning widely as the skirt slips off my hips and falls down to the floor where I lift it in the tip of one foot and kick it away, eliciting a moan from one of the boys at the door. I'm so glad they appreciate my curves.

I dance to a silent beat. Waving my arms in the air I pump my hips simulating sex. I'm completely nude but the alcohol has made me forget my tummy related inhibitions. I think the guys like all my curves anyway as suddenly I feel a set of hands on my hips and a rough denimed crotch pressed into the fold of my ass. Lips kiss the back of my neck and I shimmy against the hard body behind me. The other man comes over to stand in front of me. We dance; his crotch against my crotch, his chest rubbing against my tits. Only now I realise he's shed his top already and his hands are working on the front of his pants.

The guy behind me moves his hands then I hear the rustle of material and the metallic zing of a zipper. I can only assume he's eager to catch up with his friend.

My naked flesh presses between that of two hard, fit young men is probably the most intensely erotic thing I have ever experienced. The dancing fluidity of our bodies is so sexy. I feel fully turned on again ready to take whatever these two have for me, hmmm, maybe three if Joey can arouse his interest again.

I kiss soft, full lips and feel others trailing over my shoulders. Two hands from behind grasp and squeeze my breasts and the lips in front of me kiss down to nip and nibble on the proffered nipples. I can feel the cock pressing into my buttocks hardening and throbbing, its hot length pressing in between my globes in all it's sheathed glory. Joey had obviously handed out condoms when I wasn't paying attention. This could have been at any point really because I'm thoroughly distracted by being the filling in a hot guy sandwich. . The lips of the slim guy before me sink deeper, over my belly, to tease at my lips. I'm amazed and highly turned on by the feel of a man's mouth caressing the entrance where another man just fucked me.

I gasp when the tongue slips into me. I feel hands pulling apart my thick lips, and the pressure on me buckles my knees, which gives the cunnilinguist a better opening. He darts his tongue deeper into me, obviously enjoying my flavour. His lips and tongue flick up and down, lapping at my wet, aroused flesh. He sucks on my exposed pleasure core and causes me to shake with arousal. The man behind wants in on the action and sits down on the end of the bed, pulling me down on top of him.

His cock impales me. I sink down and enjoy the fullness I experience,and the stimulation of a mouth on my clit. It's amazingly erotic to have a man suck you whilst another is inside of you, the idea of his lips so close to the other guys pounding cock cannot fail to arouse. The sucking continues on until I scream out, squeezing the cock inside me, and flooding it with my juices. At that point, the cunnilinguist decides on a change, and stands up.

He picks up a large heavy textbook and stands on it. Then he adds another to the pile, bringing his cock to the level at which I can suck it. I give him the oral pleasure he deserves. Licking the tip of him briefly accustoms me to his unique musky taste before the cock thrusts into my mouth. The cock in front of me and the dick inside me set up a rhythm between them, tearing me apart then concertinaing me together again. Over and over they thrust and I hear their curses and moans while they take their pleasure. I growl around the meat that's filling my mouth. I am in sexual heaven. My lips cause the young lad before me to hold very still and pump his load down my throat, just then the guy below me screams and jackhammers hard making the bed shake as he forces the orgasm from him, yelling his release that fills my body.

Chapter 17

It's amazing how a threesome can invigorate a girl, and suddenly I find myself out of the post Nick Casey flunk I'd found myself in. Actually, part of the process might have been seeing him as one of the entrants for this year's *I'm famous, help me escape,* and reading that already his flagging career was taking off again. I bet someone will be his kinky jungle mistress - what great publicity.

Even the prospect of attending another wedding as a single can't dampen my good mood, even the fact it's my father's wedding to his child bride is only marginally annoying. I'm surfing on the hopes of fit blokes, free alcohol and sex, sex and more sex. Woo hoo. Okay I know it might not be healthy to be this fixated on getting laid but what else do I have in my life? My job is boring, my Mother is mostly drunk and my Dad is busy making himself a new family. Sex might be transient but it's fun while it lasts.

And I know I look good. New, bright blue satin dress, tight in all the right places and flowing in others. Classically cut, fashionably expensive and very, very sexy. The tightness and flatness of the material allows for no underwear underneath, it would ruin the line of the whole look. Well, that's my excuse and I am keeping to it.

Add a hundred pound matching handbag and even more expensive kitten heels and I am on a promise, there is no way I'm not going to score today.

My good mood even allows for me to arrive to the wedding ceremony only a few minutes late. I slip in the back, happy to not have had to do the dutiful daughter bit at the door, whilst everyone gawks on. Including whichever section of the press my father had granted exclusive rights too. Yes, he was in a band once and yes, you'd know which I'm just not going to tell you because I'm sick of being labeled simply for being his daughter.

The ceremony is quick and crappy. She's wearing something in ivory, straight and expensive with a light, floaty veil and Dad is in a black tux, looking old compared to his soft skinned, doe eyed bride.

Men in the chapel all wear the same smirk that says "Lucky bastard, I wish I were him, she's half his age. Right on!" whereas the women are looking far more solemn like they are attending a funeral, saying goodbye to another sweet fertile girl to a dirty old pervert with money. They all secretly wish they were her, though - even those a couple of decades too old to fulfill the brief.

The reception is in an expensive hotel, her choice not his then. My Dad is tight, tighter than tight in fact. I think Scrooge is one of his ancestors. It's tacky in a minimalist way. It's just like that to show off how much money they've spent. You can only get this kind of spare bareness by spending a lot of money.

I'll not have any of this crap at my wedding. Red roses, big, big wedding gown and a damn good disco and DJ. Everything else will just be trimmings. Including the husband, no doubt. I don't think love exists - at all. I think it's all just levels of greed. Greed, want and selfishness. Those who stay together only do so because they continue to get what they need from their partners. Those who divorce, get it, take it, then fuck off with it - leaving broken hearts, houses and children behind them.

But I'm not bitter.

At least the effervescent Jenny has seated me next to her younger and hotter brother, John. He's tall, skinny and blond, with the cutest smile that I've seen in a long while and he's coming on to me so strong that I am resisting, for the sheer fun of it, seeing just how far he will go to snare me. I'm not going to tease him much more, after dessert, I'm his.

Excusing myself, I stand up. I rest my hand on his shoulder as I walk past, and I know he'll follow me. Down the corridor I feel a hand on my arm, and I swirl around into his hard body.

His lips meet mine with a thud, and our alcohol laced breaths collide and combine as our bodies meld together.

I pull away, grab him by the hand and drag him along the corridor with me, giggling all the way to the disabled toilet. Opening the door I push him in then follow. I shut the door behind us. It's not a pretty space, it smells of floral disinfectant but it's big, private and the closest thing to hand.

Actually, his cock is the closest thing to my hand, and I squeeze it through the rough material of his cheap pants, then lower the zip while he lifts my infinitely more expensive dress and finds I'm not wearing knickers. No words, all action. I rub my breasts against his rough cotton shirt and he places himself between my thighs.

"Hold on," I gasp, snap open my expensive bag and pass him a condom. "Put this on then fuck me."

He didn't argue. He slipped into the cover then rammed his cock into me.

No finesse, no foreplay, but who fucking cares? I'm wet, horny and filled with hard cock and I'm more than happy with the strength of this young virile erection pounding into me. I hook my feet around his hips and my hands around his neck and hang on for dear life.

There's no explosions for me but that of satisfaction at feeling another load shooting inside me and knowing it's from my new step mother's brother. He pulls out, I straighten my skirt, blow him a kiss and leave him there panting.

"I'll have to go now, Dad." I breeze back into the room and over to my father, who looks well on his way to totally sloshed already.

"Oh, do you have to sweetheart?"

"Yeah, I need to get home, I have work to do this weekend." Now that's complete bullshit, but a pretty believable excuse.

"Oh alright then, don't work yourself to hard. Erm, Jenny and I want to tell you something before you go, though."

"She's pregnant. I know."

"How?" he asks, flabbergasted.

"Someone told me, and you can see her stomach sticking out." Father still looks completely stunned.

"Oh, well, oh, OK then."

I've really taken the wind from his sails, and before he can make any kind of scene over it, I kiss his cheek and hurry away. On the way to the door I spy Jenny and I grin wickedly. I walk up to her, embrace her, them lay my hand on her stomach,

"Congratulations!" I exclaim. "I'd given up on having brothers and sisters at my age."

She smiles awkwardly then turns to the other people around me.

"Yes, I was just about to tell you, Mum and Dad."

The looks on their faces are priceless. I've well and truly dropped her in it. Ha!

"But Dad - please - No!" I walk to the door with the noise of two grown men scuffling behind me, accompanied by the impassioned sobs of the bride.

Oops. I didn't really mean to cause such a fuss, but oh well, I'm not going to eat myself up with guilt over it. She should have told her parents earlier. I just hope their son doesn't tell them that I took his virginity, or I might be really in trouble.

Chapter 18

Mr. & Mrs. P Harbottle cordially invite you to a Halloween masque Ball. Fancy dress and Mask required. Friday 31st October from 8pm. RSVP

Oh, a fancy dress ball! Fantastic. I love fancy dress and the mask thing will be great fun, yes. Masked flirting is almost more fun than face to face flirting. The extra mystique is intoxicating. I even have a mask, it's lovely. Small, sparkly and sexy in red, which curves up the side of my face, delicately and elegantly. I used it once at a party years ago but kept it because of its beauty.

Now just to do some net surfing to work out what to wear with it. I want sexy, nope not wonder woman. And I want something a bit different so not a horny devil either. I need sophisticated but not poncy, so no I don't like that Elizabethan look.

Now that's the one! Just perfect, sexy, different and cool. Also I'm almost certain to get laid. Maybe someone will even offer to pay me; I've always been turned on by the thought of being a prostitute. This is a classy wild western whore with the frilly dress hiked up to one side exposing a red and black lace garter, and a cute little hat and red slippers. It looks as if the balconette top will show off my breasts to perfection.

And it will make old Sheila gawp and sigh and gossip. Oh yes, I am ordering this outfit, that's for sure. I'm going to be the Belle of the ball.

Knocking on the door at the Harbottles', I grin to myself, pleased as punch with my beautiful ensemble. I know that the mask doesn't hide my identity amazingly well, and I think most people I meet who know me already will know who I am. It's the strangers that I'm really interested in, as I'm feeling very horny tonight, again. I thought your hormones were meant to settle down as you got older? I swear I am hornier in my thirties than I've ever been before.

"Hello." Sheila opens the door, all smiles in her oh so predictable black cat ensemble. Her expression goes from fake smile to real shock and horror in a fraction of a second, transforming my benign plastic smile into something far more vibrant and emotive.

"Good Evening, Caitlyn. That *is* an interesting costume." I can see her gaze taking in everything from the gaudy red slippers, the knee high fishnets and revealed garter up to the tight cinched chest, and the bounty of my cleavage frothing over the top. She is well and truly appalled. I'm loving this costume more by the minute.

When I walk into the large dining room I feel lots of stares upon me. I gaze around and see all kinds of costumes, some people I recognise some I don't and others I think are really strangers. Pumpkins, Supermen and Wonder Women are mixed in with vampires, ghosts and animals with a liberal sprinkling of fairies and genies. I am so very glad to see the level of costume imagination in others nowhere challenges my costume.

I knew I'd be the Belle of the ball.

"Caitlyn, is it you?" Mr. Majors in his suit walks over and takes me hand, squeezes it briefly then drops it his eyes looking over my body as he does so.

"It is me." I smile and he grins lewdly, which is kind of disconcerting when the man is old enough to be my Grandfather.

"By Jove it is! Well I must say I do like your costume, it's very, erm, flattering." He grins nervously, his round face flushing to hot red, his eyes starting to bulge.

"What have you come as, Mr. Majors?" I ask politely, and he replies. "A politician. I dress up like one every damn day so I don't see why Halloween should be any different. Dear old Henri tried to convince me to wear something else, but I said to her, I'll be dammed if I'm going to wear some dandy costume at my age!" As if summoned by the mention of her name, Dear old Henrietta arrives by Mr. Majors' arm. She's dressed like a politicians wife I think, as I cannot detect anything costume like about her outfit.

She holds conversation with me for only a second before hurrying her husband away obviously worried about the effect of my costume on his blood pressure. I hold in a snort of laughter as they waddle away together, arm in arm. Please Lord, if you're out there, save me from that. I don't want to grow old at all, but please don't make me frumpy and senile as well!

My outfit attracts all kinds of looks from glares of icy hatred to red hot leers of lust. I dance to the middle of the road pop music being piped into the overly grand, understatedly decorated dining room. Several men come forward to dance with me, many of whom are soon after dragged away by wives and girlfriends.

Whilst stood in the corner sipping at a glass of water a cowboy slips by me, his hand rests briefly on my hip and I catch a hint of a sweet citrus smell. I decide it's worth playing a little with this one, so I spin around and meet him eye to eye.

"You can't touch, what you've not paid for, you dirty rotten good fer nothing' cowpoke. Just 'cos I'm a whore doesn't mean I'm easy you know!"

He smiles sardonically. His lips lifting at the corners and making his eyes sparkle under the wide, black sash across them. His face is further shadowed by the wide brim of his dark brown and battered cowboy hat.

"Well, excuse me Ma'am. I was just being friendly like, are you always this mean to potential customers?" his hand rests on his hip, as the elbow of his other arm rests on the bar. His body is bent towards me, one knee directed right at my crotch.

"No, but I'm always this mean to men who touch without asking a lady's permission first."

"I'll remember that in future ma'am." He grins, his fake American accent stretched, but still sounded pretty convincing. I like the look he has too, faded blue jeans, brown cowboy type boots and a plain, midnight black shirt, open at the collar.

"Good." I nod curtly then sidle up beside him, rubbing my body along the length of his. "Now, buy me a drink, and we can talk about this potential custom of yours."

"Oh, so now you're friendly enough. What would you like to drink darlin'?"

"Scotch, on the rocks." I reply, keeping to my character, and getting in some extra American Dutch courage. Knocking back the whiskey in one go might have been a bad decision though. I'm glad I went with the waterproof mascara tonight.

"Are you alright, darlin'?" He pats me on the back, as I splutter and pushes over a glass to me.

"Yep, it just went down the wrong way." I smile crookedly and take a sip of the proffered water.

"I thought so." The mysterious cowboy comments a smirk lingering over his lips. "Now then, what are your rates?"

"Oh well, I'm quite expensive, but I am very good value for money. I've never received any complaints."

"That's good because I don't buy no cheap rubbish you know, I like quality. I like to buy something I know will last." He grins once more and I smile sweetly back.

"No worries there, love. I can last as long as you need me too and longer no doubt."

He laughs out loud startling the rotund vampire behind him and making me chuckle too. Something about this guy is really hitting all my spots, and I'm pretty certain that's not just the scotch talking.

"Well, I'm definitely interested in making a purchase. Now, where do I go to get my goods?" His hand slips onto my arm and rests just above my elbow, I press closer to him.

"Well, I don't think we'll be able to get a room in this establishment, where would you suggest?"

" I'm resting my horse not far from here, and I have what I think would be a comfy work environment for you there within -what do you say? Wanna ride pillion with me?"

"As long as you promise to hold me tight and not let me fall." I reply, grazing his cheek with my highly stained lips.

"Fantastic." He knocks back the end of his drink then offers his arm to me. I take it and allow him to walk me away from this little town bar, full of little town people to a place of mystery, magic and hopefully, ecstasy.

Just at the exit he stops suddenly. "Ah, just wait here for me, my sweet lady, I've left my lasso in the hostelry, I'll be back soon."

I stand in the doorway and am partially aware of a conversation happening in the hallway with a masculine voice I vaguely recognise.

"Ahhhh Mike, I'm glad you made it."

"Hello Sheila, it's good to see you but I must be going, I have a taxi waiting for me outside."

"Love the costume, it's wild! I hope you rustled up some fun in it whilst you were here."

"Yes, yes I did thanks. OK, I've got to go now, thanks!"

And suddenly mysterious cowboy is back at my elbow, with an actual lasso in his hand.

"I hope you know that using that thing will cost you extra," I harrumph, a suggestive curve to my mouth.

"Ahh, don't worry Ma'am, I'd worked that one out. I've got extra gold from the bank to cover the surcharges."

We giggle and fall into each other's arms then into a waiting taxi. I fuzzily wonder if that guy in the hallway would be pissed off at us taking his cab but the lips of my masked stranger find my own and stop that line of thought in its steps.

These lips are confident lips making mine shiver with lust, quivering with awe at how masterfully they kiss me into submission. They make my body melt and ache just with a few second of lip to lip contact.

"Well." He hisses, our lips parting, his accent getting shakier by the moment. "I'm liking the free taster."

"Erm, who said it was free mister, I'm adding up your tab in my mind you know."

"I'd best hold back on the tasters then, hadn't I?" He grins, "I don't want to use up all my gold before I get off the damn horse."

"I thought you were rich, mister cow poke."

"Why, I am lady, but those kisses must be worth a small fortune, I best go easy on them."

I smile at the flattery and snuggle into his chest; resting a hand on his thigh and feeling something twitch higher up the leg, in the confines of the denim. The taxi ride isn't long, and I'm soon standing outside on the pavement looking at a very impressive home.

"My, my, my, this is a fine watering hole you've brought me to," I crow, clapping my hands together, mocking the actions of a giggly girl.

"Only the best for my whores." He grins, making the word whore hover in my brain, turning me on again without laying a finger on me. Tonight is going to be a good night; I can feel it deep inside my pussy.

Well, I'm glad to know you're not just a cheap cowpoke, I do like to get job satisfaction you know."

"You'll know job satisfaction alright, darlin." He growls, grabbing me around the waist and pushing his mouth against mine for a quick, intense kiss before leading the way into the darkly impressive building before us. He doesn't stop to flick on lights, just guides me with his sinewy arm along a corridor and up some stairs, then along some more corridor and through a door into a lemon-spice scented room.

I stand, waiting for something to happen as he moves smoothly and unhesitant around his room. A scratch, a spark and a flame illuminate the room slightly, letting me see the location of the dark wood bed, the light playing on the carved pillars at it's four corners.

"Wowee!" I gasp, "You really splashed out here, sir." Another candle flickers into life, and the rich red of the heavy fabric swags hanging from the pillars becomes apparent.

"I told you, only the best for my ladies of the night." A clink and clatter, makes me look over to the corner of the room where he's pouring himself a drink. "Would you like one darlin'?"

"Yes please."

I enjoy the sweet sourness of whiskey mixed with soda swishing around my mouth, the coldness refreshing me. "So, sir. Now you've got me in your boudoir, what services will you be requiring from me?" I put down the glass on the chest of drawers beside me, and swirl my dress around my legs provocatively, lifting up the split side to reveal even more of my creamy flesh.

"Well, for starters, I want to feel those pretty whore lips wrapped around my cock."

The words shoot straight to my cunt, what sexual confidence to talk this way. I wonder if it's him or the costume and accent emboldening him. Although, I suspect that a man who has such an impressive bed, and candles in his room, probably is fairly sexually dominant. I'm not sure where I pull that assumption from, the whiskey is really strong.

"I think I can stretch to that sir, well, I guess it depends on the girth of the cock in question."

Without hesitation he stands, and drops his pants, revealing his dick and its impressive girth.

"Oh, I do like a challenge." I wink broadly then sink to my knees in the deep, soft carpet. I crawl over to where he's sitting. My breasts sway, enticing him and arousing me as my nipples saw across the fabric stays holding them loosely in place. He's on the edge of the bed again by the time I reach him, his own pillar erect between his thighs. Dark and inviting, there is a soft, pearl decorating the top, and as I come to my knees, I slip my tongue between my lips and lap the drop of misture off the tip of his dick. I'm rewarded by a gravely moan.

I slip my attention lower, resting my hands on his spread thighs I dip my mouth between them and press against the fuzzy balls of his testicles that wrinkle and crinkle up in pleasure when I lap and suck on the sweet folds of flesh. Whimpers can be heard, less gravel and more intense need shows through in his voice as I nibble and lick then blow delicately over the wetted area. I move onto the staff, slipping my lips higher, lapping around and up and down the underside, making him groan.

As I climb, higher reach his yelps of delight and his moan becomes more baritone when my mouth slips down his scale, swallowing his instrument whole, with very little effort.

I play him with all my skill and soul-felt lust. Just as if I were being paid, I give him the best service, lavishing attention all over his crotch, his thighs and his cock.

"Ooooh, Kay," he gasps, pulling on my hair and yanking my mouth from around his well lubricated member. "I think we better move on, darlin'. I don't want to waste my spunk down your throat, I'll save that for another time."

"Another time? What makes you think you won't be bankrupt after this one?" I purr.

"Then I shall make myself busy making more money, anything to get those sweet, slut lips around me again." He confidently replies.

Oh yes, he can talk the talk, flowing back into the offbeat American accent, his voice falls lower, digging deep into my body. The words work their charm on me, my cheeks flush with the compliment and my pussy clenches around the word "slut."

"Now then, I want to taste your produce." Taking my hand he lifts me from my knees and presses me down onto the bed. "Lie down, make yourself comfortable, I'm planning on being some time."

I lie on the sensual velvet throw, and feel his weight next to me. His hands go to my chest first and delicately unlace the front of my dress to release my breasts to the cool air. He gently palms them and my nipples grow, harden and wrinkle. He drops his rough, stubbled chin to rub across my flesh, allowing his plump lips to wrap around a nipple and suck it into complete submission. My fingers curl up of their own accord, grabbing swathes of soft velvet in my fists.

"Sweet, so sweet." His voice is his own, and sounds very English in comparison to his Texas drawl. In fact, it sounds somewhat familiar. His hand running up my thigh, and over my garter stops my thought midway, and his lips leave my breasts and I keen at the deprivation. But as he moves lower between my thighs, and I feel my skirts rucked up around my hips, the excitement melts down into other areas and the anticipation of what treats are to come take over priority in my mind.

Reverently he peels down the large, layered knickers from over my rump. They're strange underwear, but they're the bloomers that go with the outfit, and I couldn't bear to leave them out, I felt they added a lot to my character. And how often does a woman have an excuse to wear ruffled knickers?

The panties trail right down my legs and he pulls them off, throwing them to the side, then moves smoothly back up the counterpane between my thighs until his head is right at pussy height. His stomach is flat to the bed, his hair encased calves rub against my recently depilated ones, scratching up friction, exciting me even further.

I can feel his breath feathering over my thighs and the outer edges of my labia. Gently he reaches forward and I feel the tips of his fingers probing my entrance, gently prying the sticky folds of flesh apart, opening me up to his sight.

His breath hits my clit and I bite my lip with the anticipation of the moment. His fingers open me wider, stretching me a little, but not uncomfortably. His tongue dances up and down my slit, teasingly tasting me. Pressing into my hole his tongue tip curls and tastes the quality of my juices. He slaps his lips then they're on my flesh again, caressing my clit. Oh so softly he whispers kisses over my tiny mound. I lift up, wanting to feel more pressure there to satisfy my lust.

Gently he laps, licking around and over the bump, alternating with soft butterfly kisses, driving me crazy with want. I curse and bounce my hips up and down, desperate to feel more contact. A long whine of pleasure escapes my lips when eventually I get what I long for and my cowboy sucks my clit forcefully. On release, his tongue lashes across my nub and I yell at the top of my voice with the ecstasy that washes through me.

His tongue lashes up and down the entire length of my slit then his fingers slip inside me. His mouth locks back around my clit, holding onto me fast as I bounce and grind. I scream, holding on for dear life to the blankets beneath me, I feel the orgasm rip through me like air through a decompressed cabin. Everything is sucked into the orgasmic pulsing vortex, the sounds from my throat being dragged away, leaving only squeaks at the high point of sound. I clasp my thighs around his head when hot cowboy's tongue tickles out every last drop of orgasmic joy from my soul.

He gives me no time to recover. He lifts his torso to tower over mine, his arms upright by my shoulders and taking the strain to his upper body as his crotch creeps up closer to my wide spread hole. He reaches beyond me before I can say anything and pulls a crinkly packet from behind my head. He leans back on his knees and I watch him free a condom from its pack and slip it over his erection.

Our gazes lock. He reaches forward and braces his hands beside my shoulders then stops in the perfect position to fuck me. I catch my breath and his covered cock gently probes at my entrance and smoothly it slips in, stretching me so deliciously that I mewl with the renewed ecstasy flowing through me.

"Oh God," he gasps, holding himself buried deep inside of me, before he starts to move. On the top of his stroke he bumps my sensitized clit, making my cunt tingle and close in around him. He groans as I tighten and pull him deeper inside.

His arms collapse beneath him and his face ends up in my neck. His weight on my chest heightens the spasms in my cunt, his lips on my collar bone adding more tingles to my sensitized body. This causes a spark of orgasm to ripple through my body on each shallow thrust. He lifts himself back onto his arms, he is getting needier, I can tell. Harder and harder he pushes into me and I wrap my arms around him to prevent myself from being thrust away from his body.

Every lunge shakes through his frame. I can feel his muscles throbbing. I vibrate as the ecstasy floods all my senses. I don't think I've ever felt so elated before. I know I've never had this many orgasms in such a short period of time from one cock. This mysterious cowboy is really striking all the right places, if he came looking for orgasmic gold, he has surely found it.

"Yes, yes, yes oh fuck yes," he yells. He beats harder into me then he stills. His body held out like that of an ice dancer finishing his set. Straight and straining, his head thrown back, his hips thrust into me and his toes flat against the bed. He holds the pose the only thing moving is his dick pulsing inside me.

He falls from his figure skating finery onto my chest panting and puffing. He nuzzles into my neck and I wrap my arms around him, protectively. I rub my hand up and down his back and instinctively kiss the centre of his forehead, just above his black mask.

Usually, once the sex is done. I can't wait to disengage limbs and go. I'm not a clingy girl at all. Yet right now, I could lie here forever. His strong, wiry frame cradled into my feminine softness. His powerful arm wrapped over me, his lips gently kissing the curve of my neck. I want to break the silence with a joking comment, least part of me does, but I cannot bring myself to disturb this tableau of sweet satiation.

I must have drifted off to sleep because I feel like I'm waking when his body moves off mine.

"Damn man, you knocked me unconscious with your lustful thrusting." Now is the time to joke and rib. He chuckles. I sit up, pulling together the strings of my dress, putting away my breasts in an effort to keep them warm.

"I am terribly sorry, but I could not help myself, you lusty wench. I can see why your pleasures are in great demand." He rejoins with a wide, cheeky grin.

I tap my hair and wink at him. "Thank you," I preen, "I am the best, as you now know."

"God yes," he replies, his accent turning English again, then back in his Texan drawl as he asks me how I'll be travelling back to the bordello.

"Call me a coach." I demand with a dismissive wave of the hand, "You can afford to add it on top of the bill for my services."

He leans over me and I notice his mask is still firmly in place but his hat is missing. His hair is thick and lustrous and arouses some kind of memory in me that I cannot quite put my finger on.

"Yes, hello. A taxi from fifty two Westborough place please. Yes, to fifteen Blenheim heights. Five minutes? Oh that'd be great. Thanks, thank you, bye."

"Your coach will be here soon my lady. Let me escort you to the lobby."

I take to my feet and wobble slightly so his hand comes round to steady me.

"All the blood drained from my head to other parts of my anatomy then, I think." I grin and he squeezes me.

"Well, I must say, you're the best whore I've ever laid. Thank you for your services."

We're standing in the impressive stone doorway of his home, looking out for the ordered taxi. He's laid a heavy, tartan blanket over my shoulders to keep me warm, his arm is looped around my waist.

"My pleasure," I smile, then I get cheeky again, "Least it will have been once you've paid me." I tap my foot and he bellows a laugh.

"Hang on, ma'am, I'll just going and get it." He walks back into the hall and I hear him fishing around inside some kind of vase, the gentle "ting" echoing through the large hall.

He walks over to me and I hold out my hand palm up. He places a few round things in my upturned palm then closes my fist around them.

When he lets go, I look down and several golden coins sparkle up at me.

"Why, you are generous." I smile. "I'll have to do you more often."

"Oh yes," He drawls, "Oh yes, you will." and although the words echo somewhat menacingly around the marbled hall I feel a shudder of desire which intensifies when he leans in for a kiss. It develops from a tight lipped thanks to a tongue whipping, desire fuelling kiss that has me suddenly ready to fuck once more.

A beep behind us makes me jump, and I realise it's my taxi and no more fucking will be had tonight. Cowboy walks me over to the cab. He takes the blanket from around my shoulder as he opens the door for me. Once I am in and settled he closes it to.

I roll down the window and stick my head out to blow him an extravagant kiss before disappearing down the drive away from his sight. He waves in return. I swear I can see the moonlight glinting off his teeth when he smiles but maybe that's the whiskey talking.

Chapter 19

I wake, and feel the unusual constriction around my waist then around my face. I wonder for a moment, trying to regain my bearing then blink into the bright November sunshine as it pours through my window. As my eyes adapt to the over-abundance of light I look down and things begin to stir in my memory. Ah, costume! Halloween party, mysterious cowboy.

I must have been so tired when I got in I just collapsed on the bed still clothed, without even drawing the curtains. The light dawns, too damn brightly for my delicate head so I stand up, well on the second attempt I manage it, and pull the curtains together. I shroud my room into comforting shadows once more.

I lie back, my mind spinning, my head throbbing and my stomach feeling like a shook up snow globe but yet, I smile. I have a hangover and my body is completely out of whack with the world, but my heart doesn't seem to care. I seem to be floating in euphoria. I think it's euphoria. It's not orgasmic, it's not the satisfaction of trouble well set and left behind nor is it the high that is achieved through making it to something I want. I don't know whether this is just some kind of strange illness, where all kinds of endorphins are racing for my brain while my body slowly dies.

Maybe I'm just not used to drinking so much scotch. Maybe it's the whiskey that makes it seem like last night's sex was something out of this world. I'm not convinced though because alcohol tends to make the sexual experience worse not better, and I doubt Scotch has some special ingredient missing in other alcoholic beverages, unless he dissolved a Viagra in mine.

Damn it, however you look at it, last night was bloody good. Fucking good even, amazingly fucking good in fact. Maybe it was the masks, the hidden identity thing. I don't know who he was, and I'm sure he doesn't know me either.

This is a bugger becauseI think I could get used to that kind of sex, even if it meant putting this mask on a lot.

I reach round the back of my head and slip the mask off my face. My cheeks feel naked and tingle with the relief of pressure. I wouldn't mind dressing up if it ended up in that many orgasms each time. I can think of all kinds of man/whore dress ups we could do, from way back when to the modern day. Yes, I'm sure it could work, if only I could meet up with him again.

Now then, if I could remember what his address was I might find him in the phone book, or I could call round out of the blue, but he'd not recognise me, unless I wore my costume, which I could do - a long coat and nobody but me would know. But what if he doesn't want another round? What if he just rejects me outright, I mean the sex was amazing for me, I dunno if it was anything special for him. It could have been pretty average in his opinion, I just don't know.

Also, what if I turn up and I see him out of costume and he just doesn't do anything for me? I mean, I know he's not massive. He's wiry and thin, with longer hair than I'd normally enjoy. What if he's kinda ugly with bad dress sense or something? I couldn't be doing with that at all, then he might want to fuck me, but I'd not be able to bear it. I guess I'm just going to have to accept it as a one night stand, damn it.

It's not as easy as I'd like though. All day I thought about him and I mooned about the house on Saturday and again on Sunday, whatever I did, whatever I do, images of him and what he did to me, jump to my mind unbidden. I'm even throwing myself into doing some actual work today and that's not at all like me. It's not working either, the minute the problem is solved; the cowboy pushes into my mind again.

I'm not sleeping properly, not eating properly, I'm even grumpier than usual because of this and I can't stop thinking about the sex we shared. The way he licked my cunt teasing me till I exploded, the way he nibbled my body as he thrust into me, the girth of his cock, how it fitted me so precisely, so rightly, like we were made to fit together.

If the damn images won't leave me alone, I'm going to have to go round to his house and confront him. At least a rejection or finding an ugly bloke would give me some, oh what do the Americans call it? Closure. That's it, closure.

I'll give it a few more days first; the effects might wear off after a bit of time, that's better than making a fool of myself just to finish this mental torture isn't it?

Ice cream - it works after a break up, and this has been a break up of sorts, so it should work now. I hope so, because I can't stand being this scatterbrained for much longer, I can't focus on anything and that drives me wild.

Maybe I'm sick? Penny asked me if I was OK before, so I went to look in the mirror in the bathroom and I definitely looked sick. Ghostly pale skin, bags under my eyes that a dustman would happily pick up then there was something wrong about my eyes too, they seemed to be all glazed, and dulled. I might have picked up a virus from the masked man, and maybe these thoughts of him are all fever induced. It could be true, I guess.

It never fails, the moment I want to languish in my baggy, tartan pyjamas and just watch trash on TV and eat junk straight from the carton, someone knocks on the bloody door.

"What do you want?" I scowl when I discover Mike on my doorstep.

"To come in, please."

I sigh and roll my eyes but open the door and sarcastically beckon him in.

"Come on in, sit down, make yourself at home why don't you?"

"Why thank you, I will." He grins, and seats himself on the end of my sofa.

"So, why are you here? Not to send me on a further guilt trip I hope. I see Nick in the paper and on the news almost daily now he's in the jungle with the other has-beens."

"Oh, no. This visit is nothing to do with him at all. No it's to do with what happened at Halloween."

"Erm, what happened at Halloween?" My face is etched with confusion, and he smiles.

"Oh I'm sure you remember ma'am." he puts on a fake American accent and he sounds just like - no. It can't be.

"How did you find out about that?" I growl, "Do you know the cowboy guy, did he tell you all about it in the pub the next day? Did you set it all up?"

Questions are rolling round my brain and flowing out of my mouth with the anger that Mike just seems to automatically generate within me.

"No, Caitlyn. It was me. The cowboy was me." He reaches down into a large bag on the floor and pulls out a battered cowboy hat and a lasso.

"No. It wasn't you. It couldn't have been. This is a joke, this is a revenge trick to get me back for losing you your job."

"Nope, it was me Caitlyn, come on. Think. How did I know your home address without you telling me? Didn't you hear Sheila talking to me in the hall of her house before we left and surely you picked up on my accent. I dropped the American often enough."

My eyes stretch wide, my mouth is lolling open and my brain is working overtime.

"It was you, wasn't it?" I shake my head as he nods his and I start to assimilate all this. Maybe he did give me some kind of skanky virus. No wonder I've felt so weird since the party.

"I was the rich cowboy, and I've brought some more coins in the hope that I could use your services again." The mock Texan rolls over my senses and the chocolate coins clatter down onto the coffee table.

"No." I reply standing up and backing away. "No, just no."

I can't juxtapose the two images to rest the same. Mike is an annoying stick of a man who has done nothing but drive me crazy since I first met him. He can't be the mysterious cowboy who gave me the fucking of my life.

"I know it's a lot to take in," he stands up and walks towards me, "but I thought you knew it was me from the beginning."

"No, I had no idea at all. I thought you were a stranger. I didn't think I'd meet the cowboy ever again."

I'm horrified to feel a tear rolling down my cheek, and more horrified when he wraps his arms around to hold me and I recognise the embrace. I feel the same comforting excitement as I did in the arms of my mystery cowboy. I push hard against his chest, my eyes blazing, pushing myself away from him.

"You tricked me, you dirty bastard." I scream, my hands tightly fisted at my side.

"No, Caitlyn." His eyes show hurt, like a child who's been denied a treat.

"Yes, you tricked me; you put on a fake accent, masked yourself and created this persona to entrap me."

"Oh get over yourself," he spits, his face hardening. "I did no such thing. I dressed up, went to the party then you came on to me."

"I came on to you?" I laugh harshly.

"Yes, you started it and I thought you'd forgotten our differences. I was willing to do so too." Mike snaps back.

"I didn't know who the hell you were, I'd have not offered my services if I had known." I throw my hands in the air and turn on my heel not able to look into his burning copper eyes any more, disconcerted by the memories of those eyes in the mask, his body over mine.

Mike's hand lands on my upper arm and spins me round to face him.

"But you did. We fucked. You sucked my cock, I licked your sweet pussy and you flooded my face with your juices. I fucked you, and you fucked me and I've never felt like that before."

I strain away from his grip, but the fingers tighten, he's probably bruising me with his grip.

"I know, and it makes my stomach turn." I growl right into his face, one step away from spitting at him. His lips hit mine before I'm even aware of what's happened. His mouth encapsulates mine and I try to fight him away but he presses harder against me until my lips buckle under the pressure. I reluctantly allow his tongue entrance where it dominates me, enflaming my blood with lust, which starts to flush out the anger. I begin to melt. I try to struggle away from his strong arms and his demanding kiss but I can't. He's holding me to him so tightly I feel he might squeeze me into a tight ball.

I reach up to try and pull him away from me. I grab hold of the back of his shirt, but instead of ripping and pulling him back my rebellious hands lie there and refuses to let me part my body from the anticipated ecstasy.

I can't remember why I was so set against this a moment a go. A little voice in my mind tries to yell at me "It's Mike, oh but it's Mike, you can't. He's got no job, he's annoying. Caitlyn, Caitlyn No!" But the voice whispers away into nothing as I'm carried along by the heat of his kiss, the memory of my cowboy leaping up to the fore- front of my mind. If I just don't open my eyes and look at Mike I can happily remember it's my cowboy. I can't meld the two, though.

This thought stuns me into action and I do manage to pull his body away from me.

"No, I can't do this with you."

He waves his arms in the air.

"But you already have, for God's sake Caitlyn. Why can't you accept it?"

How do I explain to him how much I'd decided I didn't like him, how much antipathy I'd built up to him over the last months? I can't possibly, because it just shouts out as a total lie when compared to the amazing action of the weekend past. How can I hate someone I shared so much ecstasy with?

"Do I have to dress up like a damn cowboy? Do I need to get my mask? Would you be with me then?" He grasps the wisps of hair at the side of his head and growls. "I can't wait any longer Caitlyn, I don't just want you, I need you. I've gone mad thinking about you. I thought it'd just be a one night thing, but I can't get you out of my mind. Caitlyn, please."

I look into his eyes and I can see the depth of emotion there and it tugs at something deep inside me. It frightens me how easily he can make me melt, how he can make me want to fuck him. I don't like this, I don't like how I'm floundering, not knowing what will happen next. I don't like how he seems to know me so well, yet he doesn't know me at all.

I'm frightened and like a scared dog I bare my teeth and stand my ground.

Shaking my head violently I scream. "No!" I stare at him, seeing that wounded look in his eyes for a second before he strides over to me and slams me up against the wall.

"Stop behaving like a spoilt fucking brat," he growls and kisses my cheek and my lips. "You want me, I know you do. I can feel it, see it in your eyes."

I struggle and strain, but he is deceptively strong and keeps hold tight of my wrists, pining them down at my sides while his mouth roams over my face, under my ear and down on to my neck.

"No, no, no. Stop, Mike stop." I sob out loud, my body torn apart by the arousal and my denial of it. I don't know what to do. His lips ignite me and I want to be with him, I want to give in and just go with my instincts but everything that I've built up to keep me safe from the world is straining to keep Mike well away from my vulnerable heart.

"No, I'm not going to stop. I know you don't want me to, your body is craving for me. Just listen to it, listen to your body." He nibbles my neck and I strain to move my hands.

"Oh, we're not going to get anywhere like this." He pulls me away from the wall and drags me by one wrist towards the bedroom, scooping up his bag on the way.

I slap his hand with my free one, then try to pry his fingers apart, but he squeezes me tighter.

"Ow, Mike, no, not in there. No, Nobody goes in there but me, Mike no!" But he clicks open the bedroom door and drags me in.

"Oh stop your whining, it's a bedroom. It's made for fucking."

Yes, it's a bedroom, yes I know it's where most people fuck, but I don't. I just don't like people going into my room. It's my private place, reserved only for me, and now Mike is stood in the middle of it, tainting it with his personal vibes.

He pushes me down to the bed then straddles my waist, both my hands clasped in one of his at the wrist. With the other hand he picks up the flexible lasso, and winds it round my wrists and the metal of the brass bed head. He leans up and watches me struggle to get free.

"Right." He exhales, slipping down my body, holding my legs together between his strong thighs. His fingers work open the top button of my pyjama top, then move down to the next one, until the buttons are all open and he pulls the tartan material apart, revealing my breasts, I'm rather distressed to notice my slutty nipples are already erect. He must have noticed it as well. His lips descend to suck upon them.

"Mike!" I gasp. It's meant to be a protest, but I just love what he's doing to me. Damnit, I can't deny it. He excites me in a way no other man has ever done before. He makes my body tremble with just a glance. His lips only have to touch any part of my skin to make my pussy shudder with sexual pleasure.

Even the constriction of the lasso holding me to the bed turns me on. I'm completely at his mercy. It's frightening to be this out of control, but like a rollercoaster ride, the adrenaline of fear is giving me such an amazing buzz that I can't stand it.

As if he understands I've come to some kind of agreement with myself, he slips himself between my legs, kissing my stomach, making me giggle when he dips his tongue into my belly button. Grasping the elasticated band in both hands he pulls down and I lift up my bottom off the bed, to aid him, definitely showing I'm not going to protest any more.

He looks at me and once the trousers have been pulled off my legs he lets out a shuddering sigh.

"I'm not going to force you to do something you don't want, Caitlyn." He slips his hands down the side of my body, resting it on my hip. "So if you don't want this to go any further just tell me now. I'll untie you and leave."

I don't speak. My tiny internal danger alarm screams at me to shout up, all the reasons for not letting him near me running round and round my brain but I still don't speak. I can't give up on this kind of ecstasy. I've got to go further, I've got to find out why it happens, how it happens and if it was only a one off. Curiosity may have killed the cat but I'm giving in to mine, I can't possibly do anything but.

His hands leave my skin and he moves off the bed. I wonder if he might unstrap me but the sparkle in his eye tells me I won't be released. I'm not sure what I feel about that, I don't know if I like this, but I know I don't hate it. It's uncomfortable, it's unknown territory, but I am still excited, aroused and salivating at the sight of him undressing.

His chest is well defined, a surprise for his frame, his shoulders are broad and sexily curve down into his sparsely haired muscular chest. His stomach is firm, but with a little curve of fat goodness. I like a bit of flesh there as a pelvis bone grating against me is not at all arousing.

He unbuckles his belt and unzips his jeans. I run my tongue over my lips, watching the trousers slide down his tight thighs and over his masculine calves. His boxers follow dropped casually to reveal the bobbing bulge beneath.

It looks just as magnificent in the less forgiving artificial lamp light as it did in the candle lit splendour of Halloween. He picks a condom from out of his pocket and slides it effortlessly over his cock. I enjoy the visual feast as he strides over to my bed and lies down beside me. He strokes from my chin over the curve of my breast and down my stomach to my thigh.

His lips grasp my earlobe and pull, eliciting a soft moan for the discovery of a new erogenous zone. His mouth continues down the side of my neck, to the cup of my collar bone and onward. His weight shifting he reaches over and tastes my breasts, one hand manipulating one, whilst his teeth torture the other.

I feel it all at once confining and liberating to be unable to move my hands. I can't direct his movement. I can't touch him or give him pleasure. I just have to lie here and take it. All I can do is concentrate on my pleasure, that's a great joy. He kisses on over my stomach and into the down of my pubis. I know where he's going and arch up my hips, spreading my thighs and inviting him in, letting him know that I want him, the keening noise letting him know that I need him.

He drops lower covering my folded lips with tight lipped kisses then his tongue wriggles out and parts me before lapping up and down, mopping up the pooling liquid therein. I wriggle and writhe lifting myself up to him, offering him the pearl of my pleasure. I yell my delight when he grasps it and sucks with just enough pressure to flood my cunt with ecstasy, the spasms shaking me from tip to toe.

"I want you." he growls, coming up from between my thighs, his lips and cheeks shining with my juices. Slipping up and over my breasts he kisses me, and the taste of me on him excites me further, I lick and suck at Mike's lips, taking my nectar from him while he gently injects me with his cock. The perfect medication for the burning fever inside me.

"Oh, fuck yes," he hisses, his body rocking to and fro. "Oh, I've needed this Caitlyn. You drive me crazy with lust. You're so fucking sexy."

I blush, his compliment means a lot to me now that I have accepted him as my mysterious cowboy. Obliterating all other opinion from my mind I go on all I have discovered in the last few days. This is a man who arouses me to such heights, to such pleasurable pinnacles that I can't think of anything else, and my body craves him.

Thrusting rapidly he kisses my cheek, my neck, my chest.

"Yes." I groan, "Oh God, yes, Mike!" Speaking his name jars me for a moment but not in a bad way, in a way that excites me further. He's no longer a mystery; he's a real life person, accessible and willing. He wants me. How can it be a bad thing?

His name spurs him on and I know this won't last much longer but I don't care. I just want to feel him explode inside me, the feel of his pleasure gives me joy and as odd as it seems to me, my orgasm is not what matters here. Though the repetitive pounding of him thrusting hard into me is tickling my clit and making my cunt tingle with heat.

"Oh God, Caitlyn, yes!" Mike forcefully thrusts over and over again panting and hissing his pleasure. He slams his cock into me and shakes with orgasm. He thrusts again and again forcing it deeper and deeper into my body.

Before rolling off Mike unhooks his knot and lets my arms fall from their imprisonment. He rolls over to the side of me, and strokes up and down my body. He nibbles on my ear. I snuggle closer to him, enjoying the feel of his hard hand gliding over my soft curves.

I gasp in surprise when he strokes down to my pussy then groan with delight as the fingers dive down the soft slick slit. I'm amazed by his sure stroke. A single finger circles my nub making me mewl and keen into his shoulder, my teeth biting into his flesh as I explode.

"You wicked woman." he whispers.

"What?" I look at him, puzzled and he picks up my hand in his, and places it on his crotch. "You've gotten me all excited again."

I giggle and squeeze his cock, slipping my hand up and down it's length. "I think I can do something with this." I continue to wank him, my hand smoothing up and down his shaft, my fingers pressing at the base and smoothing up its softly distended length.

I am rewarded with a throaty growl for my efforts and I smile in satisfaction, or is it dissatisfaction? Even with the orgasm of a few moments ago I can feel the heat of sexual arousal coursing through my veins. I let go of his cock then come to my knees on top of the bedspread. I kiss him like I'm drowning and sharing his oxygen. My lips trek over his face up his nose, across his brow, down one cheek and up the other then down the slim, sexy line of his neck.

I reach out and open my bedside draw. I pull out a condom and pause in my kissing while I unroll it. I continue my ministrations and slip the condom on before I swing my leg across his middle, and using one hand I grasp him and glide him up and down my wet slit.

His moans are highly rewarding so I do it some more, up and down I sweep his erection, every time it touches my sensitive clit I writhe and spasm with the tingling pleasure that radiates through me.

"Please, please, please." he moans, his eyes shut tight, his face a mask of erotic tension and sexual want. I press him against my opening. Gently and maddeningly slowly I press him into myself. Enjoying every moment of the delicious stretching, revelling in this slow filling up, until he is stuffed inside of me.

Throbbing he sits there, waiting for me to move my body. He reaches out and grasp my hips, his fingers dig into to me and slowly I move, holding myself at the top of my arch, his cock just inside of me, its tip sitting in my warm juices. I hold it for a few seconds and watch his head thrash from side to side before I slide down again, in to the hilt.

I drop and rise three times slowly, oh so slowly before I cannot take any more of the teasing myself and begin to move my arse in a rapid-fire bouncing movement. I enjoy watching his face contort, the rapid change from oh too slow to fast, fast, fast is like sensual torture, sending his synapses into overdrive.

"Oh Fuck." His eyes flutter open and his gaze meets mine. His mouth is held in an "o" of a moan and I drop to kiss it, nibbling on the bottom lip, my gaze locked on his, feeding off the lust between us. I close my eyes when the flooding pleasure becomes too much and I reach the peak of orgasm without effort, almost without realising. It hits me like a punch, and I pause in my movement, just my pussy muscles clenching and spasming around him as I come.

Panting from the ecstasy, I begin to move, up and down again, keeping a steady, cantering pace. My heart thudding and thumping, my clit stinging deliciously at each contact with his skin. Mini orgasms wrack my body as his cock rides up and down my sensitised tunnel.

From his moans I know he's close to coming again, his face red with the strain of impending release. The sinews in his neck stand out proudly as he lifts his hips and body to meet me, to exert more and more pressure where we bang together before we recoil, only to bang together once more.

Slapping flesh sounds carry under the panting and moaning. His lips moving without issuing sound. I ram my body down onto him with all my strength. On the second such stroke he yells, his shoulders pulling up off the bed, his face scrunched up in the agonizing ecstasy of orgasm. His hands clamp around my waist and hold me still as his dick spurts inside of me. We hold like that for a moment then relax. I slip my leg over him and slide to his side, my legs tingling, my pussy throbbing contentedly.

His arm rests under my head and I curl up into his shoulder. He wraps himself around me until I am face to face with him in a strong embrace. My hands are pinned to my sides, my eyes inexplicably wet with tears.

"Thank God you only cost me chocolate coins, otherwise I'd be bankrupted paying for your services."

I chuckle and kiss his wide grin.

"Damn, you're good woman." he sighs, kissing my forehead, "I think I'm addicted to you."

I flush with pleasure, then bait him. "Addicted? After we've fucked twice?"

"Three times." He grins. "You're highly addictive. I was a goner from the first kiss."

"I just think you don't have the balls to resist me." I crow, my smile covering all my face.

"My balls don't want to resist you. They're as addicted as the rest of me."

I laugh and slap his chest playfully, enjoying this post-coital moment. It's funny, I've never had this kind of intimacy before but now I'm expecting it, needing it, almost but not quite more than I need the orgasms that come before.

"Caitlyn, have you really never let anyone in your bedroom?"

I look at him and shake my head against his arm.

"No, never. It's my personal space."

"I'm sorry for invading it." He says solemnly.

I shrug my shoulders, "Don't worry about it." Suddenly it seems like a very silly childish thing to have done, and I don't see why it was ever such a big issue.

He kisses me and smiles. "I didn't come here to force myself on you, really. You've driven me mad, to the point I just had to give in. I resisted all the way you know."

"Pardon?" I grin, wondering what he means.

"I was very annoyed at myself for enjoying our sex so much it was meant to be a revengeful one night fuck, but no, you were so damn good I couldn't get you out of my mind."

"Of course I was so damn good. You were the surprise. I was contemplating coming round just out of the blue to see you, maybe even wearing my whore's costume."

"Really?" His eyebrows rise. "I'd have liked that."

I stifle a yawn. "I really had no idea it was you, though."

"Well, yes, I kind of worked that out. Anyway, I should leave you to sleep, it's late."

"Thanks." I smile, cuddling him close then releasing him away from my body. "Do you want to go out on Friday?" I ask lifting up the bed clothes and sliding underneath.

"Yeah, cool." He smiles.

"Vincentios - my treat." I yawn, closing my eyes.

"OK, see you at seven, yeah?"

"Seven's good." I mumble, feeling his lips brush my cheek.

"Night." he whispers then I hear the click and bump of my bedroom door shutting, and the heavy thump of the front door closing behind him.

Chapter 20

"Katy! You look *molto bene* my sweet one!" Tony grins widely, and takes in the little red number I'm wearing, the plunging neckline and the swishing hem, delicately kissing the top of my knees. "My best table is ready for you. Come, come."

I follow him and seat myself, wondering where Mike is. It's weird for me to turn up to a meal before my partner. I needn't have worried, Mike comes into sight at the doorway and Tony slaps him heartily on the back then shows him over.

It's totally crazy that I have butterflies dancing in my stomach right now, and they go crazy with delight when he lays a soft kiss on my cheek.

"Hey, gorgeous," he greets me and sits down. "I hope you've not been waiting long."

"Just a few minutes." I respond with a smile.

"Good, I don't like to keep a woman in suspense for too long, a little maybe, but not too long."

My mind conjures up images of his skilful tongue teasing me to the brink of orgasm, pausing 'til I couldn't take it any longer. My cheeks flush, and I know he knows what I'm thinking.

"How are you?" I ask, eager to change the subject, my cheeks burning painfully now.

"I'm very well, thank you." We continue to chat as we chose our meals and wine. I spend a lot of time watching him. Observing the fluidity of his movements, the glint in his eye and the sweet way his hair moves and shimmies as he goes about his business.

Every move he makes reminds me of a moment in our love making, wow, did I really just think *that* term? Love making.

Well it seems so right, and as much as I could try and deny it, I know our joinings aren't just physical.

"What are you thinking?" he asks, a spoonful of ice cream slipping between his lips as he gently purses them, like he's bestowing a butterfly kiss.

"Oh, erm, nothing really." I giggle, my cheeks burning again.

"Oh come on, you can tell me." He protests.

I beckon him close with my finger, then whisper in his ear. "I was thinking about the way you make love to me."

It's his turn to flush, and I chuckle happily at his burning cheeks.

"Funnily, I was thinking the same thing. Your place or mine?"

We end up in my flat, stripping each other on the doorstep.

"Mike, let me find my key." I try and shove him away from my exposed breast, but his lips grip tighter and his teeth nibble my nipple making me groan while I fish around in my clutch bag behind his back.

One of his hands slips under my skirt and insinuates its way into my knickers. A finger snakes between my wet lips and I moan, pressing back against him. I take him off balance and managing to flip our positions so that he's against the door, and I am pressing into him. My lips find his and his hand burrows deeper between my thighs.

I remember what I am meant to be doing and as I kiss I open one eye, and try to press my key into the hole. I gasp when Mike presses a finger into my hole, and the key rolls into place in the lock. A turn and we're stumbling back into my living room, I kick out my heel behind me and catch the door, hearing it slam shut behind us.

We stumble, giggling and kissing, banging against the kitchen side, where he takes the time to rip the other breast out of my dress and bra, nibbling, kissing and nuzzling on them, around them and between them.

I lean back, my hands resting on the counter top, groaning happily. Moments later I wrap my arms around him and push him back. Laughing we stumble and his back hit's a wall. I rip down his buttons and slam open his shirt so I can run my lips all over his sweet chest. He groans as my fingers faff with his belt. I am trying to undo it but my fingers are shaking with built up lust. It takes quite a while to undo his trousers while we're rolling along the wall and I'm feeling light headed.

"Ouch, damn handle." He curses then we laugh some more and he opens my bedroom door, falling backwards onto his arse.

"Are you alright?" I gasp between giggles and he guffaws loudly, nodding his head. I bend to the floor and pull off his shoes, next come the socks then I pull off the gathered pants from around his ankles.

"Thank you." He grins reaching forward and pulling me over. I land on top of him. Quickly he rolls over and pins me to the ground.

"Ah ha, I have you now!" he exclaims and I gasp in fake fear.

"Oh, no! The nasty master has got me. Help! Helllllllp!"

He pushed his lips down on mine to silence me, his hands pressing up my skirt as I writhe below him, not very energetically though, just enough to keep playing the game. When he reaches the flimsy lace barrier of my knickers he rubs me through them. I groan at the rough texture when it grazes over my lips, and just touches the tip of my clit.

"Now wench, if you lie still, and let me do what I want, I'll make it pleasurable for ye, if you make a fuss and a fluster, I'll beatcha within an inch of your life!"

He scowls and I hold back a chuckle.

"I'll be good sir, just don't hurt me."

"That's a good girl." He says as his lips plunge down my neckline and into my cleavage. "Now, where was I?"

He kisses my stomach then holding my thighs wide he runs his tongue up and down the thin material of my panties, making me groan and sigh. I want to feel more pressure on my pleasure zones.

"Damn underwear." he grumbles then I feel two of his fingers pressing into the lace. A hard pull and I can hear the distinctive rip of material giving between his strong hands. The vibrations echoing up my thighs and into my pubis, making me gasp then bite my lip. Falling into character, I plead for him not to hurt me.

"Oh no, sweet one, I won't hurt you." he pants, his gaze fixed on my crotch. I feel his gentle probing tongue and the scratchy soft carpet itching my shoulders and buttocks. The fact that those lacy knickers cost me a lot of money and the constriction of my frock around my waist are all forgotten as he slowly and methodically brings my body to a mind shattering orgasm.

"To your hands and knees wench, come on." I pick up my quivering body and comply, my body still suffused with post orgasmic bliss.

"Oh you have a pretty rump." he coos, slapping first one buttock then the other, making me squeal with shocked delight. "I'm itching for you to be naughty so I can spank this sweet, sweet bottom. It will look beautiful in raspberry pink."

I've always thought I wasn't into pain, least not on the receiving end of it, but the way he paints the picture and the way my cheeks smart from the soft slap make me eager to be naughty, to feel his wrath meted out on my ample backside.

I hear him curse. "Condom?" He whispers.

"In the drawer."

He moves away from me and I let my mind wander to more images of being tied down and spanked. Yes, I can imagine that feeling good. To be completely at his mercy.

Just as those thoughts suffuse my mind I feel his fingers splitting my cheeks open then the rock hardness of his sheathed cock pressing against my slick hole. I groan as slowly his erection pushes in until I can feel his wiry pubic hair touching my buttocks and tickling at my anus.

I'm a virgin there, anal sex had never appealed to me before but thinking about the possibility I find myself turned on by the idea of Mike taking me there.

"Yes, oh fuck, yes." he groans and see-saws back and to on his knees, thudding me backwards and forwards, making my breasts swing and bobble beneath me. As he moves his finger seeks out my tightest hole. Gently he sweeps up the juices from my crack and presses the tip of his slick finger into me. I push back on him slowly, feeling his finger sinking deeper and popping past my sphincter.

"Oh yes, I'm so going to have to fuck this arse." he groans, his finger embedded within me. He slams harder and harder into my cunt then suddenly he pulls out. But he slips another wetted finger into my arse.

"Oh I'm going to get you so wet and stretched and ready baby. Then I'm going to feed my hard cock into this tight hole and I'm going to fuck you till we both explode."

"Oh please, Sir. Not there, your dick will split me apart."

"Pish woman," he cries, stuffing another finger into me. I gasp as my anus is stretched more than it's ever been before. "Your slutty hole can take me, and you'll enjoy it."

I bite my lip, ready for the searing pleasure pain of him pushing into my tight passage, really a little anxious knowing his girth, but trusting him not to hurt me.

"Darling," he whispers, "if it gets too much just shout out 'cowboy' and I'll stop, okay? I want this to feel good for you too."

I nod my assent.

"So tight." he hisses and he slides his erection into me, slowly, oh so slowly, giving me time to adapt. He seeks out and finds my clit with a finger and gently circles it. The pleasure centred there makes the intrusion of his cock less painful.

I grunt in a very un-lady like way as he introduces more of himself into me. The sensation of a dick inside me there is so foreign but in itself that unusual feeling is arousing. It's the attraction of knowing that this is special, something kinky.

When he's fully inside of me, he holds himself there. Gently he strokes a hand over my hip, the other hand paused over my clit before he gently pulls back and makes me gasp with the empty feeling deep inside. The joy is in the pressure releasing and I feel his fingers circling my wet clit once more when he shifts his cock back in, creating a slow rhythm. The pressing in causes erotic pain, the pulling out, pleasure. The faster he strokes in and out, the more the feelings get melded together and fuse into one whole painful pleasure experience.

"Oh fuck, oh yes, oh God, oh hell." I chant, "So intense, fuck, I can't take much more."

And I can't, I feel like I will explode if he continues to move like he is. I think I might yell out my safe word at any moment. The pressure on my clit intensifies the ecstasy but also contributes to the feeling that it's all too much. He groans, his body slapping off my buttocks and his balls teasing my slit as they swing back and to.

"Not much more." He gasps, "I'm so close, oh so close."

His thrusts get harder and wilder, his finger is so hard against my clit and the movement of our body moves is causing the friction that starts off my convulsive orgasm.

"Yes, Caitlyn, yes." I feel him throbbing inside of me as he holds himself deep inside. The heat from my clit travels everywhere and I can feel my cunt contracting around fresh air, feel the waves of it stroking the underside of his cock embedded deep inside my anal passage.

As our panting eases and the intense pleasure flows away he releases himself from inside of me, sending another jolt of relieved pleasure through my body, before I slump, achingly to the floor.

"I'm so glad I went for the thick carpet in here." I gasp rolling over onto my bottom, and examining my rubbed red knees.

"Yeah, so am I." Mike agrees sitting back and examining his own.

"You could have taken me to the bed though, a real gentleman would have." I humphed, teasingly.

"But I was a scoundrel and a rogue, not a proper gentleman at all. Plus, I couldn't wait to get at you; it's all your fault for being so God-damned gorgeous."

"Ha." My cheeks flush with pleasure at the compliment. "Smooth talker."

I get to my feet and let the dress fall from around my waist then peel off the shredded knickers. "You know, these things cost a fortune." I wave them at him, on the end of my finger, staring accusingly.

"Again," he says, snatching the material away and shoving it in his pocket of his newly pulled up pants. "It's your fault for being so sexy."

"You can't blame everything on my beauty." I stick my nose in the air in mock snobbery and he guffaws.

"Most things I can, though," he quips as I slip into my red satin nightie.

"Men." I tut and shake my head. We laugh together.

"Right, well I better get home to my bed." he smiles, "Thanks for the dinner and the lovely evening."

"My pleasure," I reply. "I'm in all weekend if you decide you want to drop by."

"I'll ring you tomorrow." He kisses me on the forehead. "Sleep well, beautiful."

I'd probably sleep better if he wasn't in my life. Things have suddenly got a lot more interesting, and I'm spending far too much time thinking. I mean, I enjoy his company, he is brilliant in the sex department, amazing even and he's entertaining and thoughtful but, he's unemployed. He's unemployed and I paid for dinner tonight. He's unemployed and I'd end up paying for dinner every night. He seems in no rush to get himself another job, and I'm not going to be in a relationship with a leech.

But then can it be considered leeching when he gives me back so many non-material things? I mean, it's not all about money is it? No, but I've seen it become about that, more times than I can count on both hands. A rich partner takes on a poor partner. It always ends in divorce, and the rich partner becoming a lot less rich.

But, what was the place he took me to when he was my mystery cowboy? He called it home, but that was not the house of an out of work PA, not even the house of an employed PA come to that. Is it his parents' house, one he's inherited or, God forbid, does he still live with his mum? I realise I don't really know that much about him.

I don't know his birth date or age; I don't know his favourite colour or food, though he said he enjoyed Italian. I don't know anything about him, nothing solid anyway. I know he's fucking hot and he makes me laugh and he inspires all kinds of things inside me, like trust. I trusted him tonight. I never trust anyone but myself, so why do I trust him? Why?

These questions aren't going to get answered tonight, but they continue to spin through my mind as I twist and turn in my sheets, trying to sleep.

Chapter 21

"Yes, that would be lovely, I'll be round at about 4 o'clock ish, is that ok? Great, what's the address again? Yeah, yep, I'm writing it down. OK, see you later, bye, bye now, bye."

So that gives me four hours to get up, get bathed and get dressed. I think I might just make it. I was surprised to pick up the phone to his voice, but pleasantly surprised, even more so when he invited me to dinner at the address he took me to when I was his whore.

I do hope he doesn't live at home with his parents, I don't think I could deal with that. But I am sure a grown man wouldn't take a whore, even just a pretend one in fancy stockings to his room if Mum and Dad were somewhere in the house. I can't work out how he could afford such a home otherwise though and it's such a big place just for one.

I could lie in bed questioning all day and never find the answer. I'd have to be patient and ask him over dinner later. That in itself is weird. A date with Mike. I hated him before. How could I change my mind so completely?

Well, I'm not in control of things and as much as I don't like it, it doesn't look like things are going to change any time soon, so if I want this thing (I can't call it a relationship, no, not yet) with Mike to last, and I'm pretty sure I do, I'll just have to wing it, and make it up as I go along.

Damnit, I do like to have a plan, and planning to just go with the flow isn't any kind of real plan now is it? Well, I guess it will have to do.

"You smell wonderful." Mike greats me at the impressive dark wood door of the building he lives in.

"Why thank you." I smile and giggle. He nuzzles into my neck then pulls me into the hall and shuts the heavy door behind us.

"It's getting cold isn't it?" I start some small talk as I take off my hat, gloves and coat.

"Oh yes, winter is definitely setting in now," he replies, taking my hand and leading me down the corridor and through a door into a room with sofas, a log fire and a big screen TV.

"Oh now that's a boy toy and a half," I exclaim, looking at the massive screen.

"Well, you've got to have your creature comforts right?" Mike laughs.

"Men and their tellies." I shake my head. "I just don't get it."

"It's the same as in all things, the bigger the better. Don't you agree with that?" I sit on a soft, red sofa that swallows me up in its comfort as I sink down.

"No actually, if it were true I'd have married Dave, he had an enormous wang. I wouldn't have looked twice at you."

He clutches his heart dramatically. "Oh, that wounded me Caitlyn, wounded me."

"Well, you did ask." I reply, giggling. "Size doesn't matter baby, nope. It's all in the way you wiggle it."

"Ha!" He sniffs. "Now you're just saying things to placate me."

"Damn you're nearly as observant as you are sexy," I reply with a wink.

"Thank you, I think." He chuckles, "Would you like a drink?"

"Tea please, milk but no sugar, I'm sweet enough."

"Tell me about it." Mike's gaze runs up and down my body. "I'll be back in a minute."

It's always weird being left in a room in someone's home on your own. I'm always torn between having a good root round and not breathing or touching anything. This room is large and the dark wood paneling makes it seem very formal, at least at first.

The deep sofas and the big TV take the edge of the olde worlde formal look. The big windows let in a lot of light, warming the room, and giving a beautiful view over a large manicured lawn and beautifully tended boarders. I give in to temptation and go and stand close to the window taking in the garden and all its beauty. The green pines stand tall and bushy against the other trees in various states of undress.

There aren't many leaves on the lawn so someone has recently cleared them all up. Reds, yellows and oranges overlap each other beneath the bigger trees and glitter in the crisp, frost laden light of the slowly setting sun.

"Beautiful isn't it?" Mike's voice comes from the door, and I look up to see him carrying two plain white, steaming mugs.

"It's gorgeous. I love autumn, and this garden shows off all the season's magnificence."

"Oh I'll be sure to tell Eli that, He's my gardener and he feels terribly unappreciated sometimes."

"He does a great job." I enthuse, taking a steaming mug from Mike's hands.

"He does well for his sixty odd years doesn't he?"

"Amazingly well." I feel Mike's arm slipping round my waist, and I enjoy the warm comfort it brings.

"Oh, he'll like you. He likes a good bit of praise, does Eli, and he'll be thrilled with it coming from such an attractive young lady."

"Oh now, you're just smooth talking me." I grin, my cheeks flushing.

"Oh, I don't think it counts as smooth talk when it's so blatantly obvious that it's the truth."

"You just want in my panties."

"If the truth gets me in your knickers, all the better." Mike replies walking over to the sofa. I follow him and sit down, thigh to thigh with him.

"Mike, can I ask you something personal?" I ask, after a little moment of silence.

"Sure." He answers, "Fire away."

I leave it a second, concentrating on the crackling of the logs in the fireplace. Trying to think of the best way to put it.

"Ok, I'm just going to ask it straight out. How come you live here? I mean you were a PA, now you're unemployed. How the hell do you afford the upkeep here?"

"I knew it'd come up eventually." he sighed, rubbing his hands around his mug.

"I've not been completely honest with you there Caitlyn. I was Nick's PA, but only because no bugger else would do it." He smiles when he sees the light of recognition in my eye, "You know what a scatter brained diva he is, no one would work with him, so in the end I gave up and did the job myself."

"If you're not a PA, what are you?" My brows knit together in confusion.

"I run the channel Nick's programme appeared on."

My jaw drops as I let that sink in.

"So you're like, the CEO of the biggest TV company in the UK?"

"Yeah, that's me." He shrugs.

"Ok, now I need to ask how old you are, either you are damn young for your job or you look bloody good for your age."

"Will you be ok having me be your sugar daddy?" His eyes glisten with cheek.

"Why, how ancient are you?" He thumps my shoulder.

"I'm not ancient. Forty on the fifth of December in fact." He grins.

"So you're young for the job, wow, I'm impressed."

"What with? My job or how old I am?"

"Oh, both. I only put you in your early thirties. You must deal with stress really well."

"Yeah, I employ someone to stress out for me." He grins, slipping his arm around my shoulder. "So do you feel better for knowing?"

"Yes, yes I do. I was worried you were after my money." I snort with laughter at how ridiculous that seems.

"Oh no, not your money, just what's in your knickers, that's all." He puts down his empty mug, and wraps the other arm around me, pulling me into his chest and caressing my back.

"Oh, well that's alright then." I snuggle into his embrace, noting how dark it's gone already, watching the flames dance in the black of the fireplace.

"I'm going to retire soon." He says and I kiss his cheek.

"At forty?"

"Yeah, I'm not enjoying it like I used to, and I have other ways to bolster my income. I'll let someone a little younger and a lot less long in the tooth take over my place."

"Wow, now there's a scoop for the tabloids." I laugh but Mike stiffens, and I realise it was a silly joke to make.

"I'm sorry, I didn't mean that. Well it was a joke. I'd never ever - I just wouldn't." I trip over the words in my eagerness to make things right.

"No, no you've gone too far." His hand squeezes my arm and his eyes don't show the same anger as his words. "You're going to have to be punished for speaking out of turn you impudent wench."

Ah, now I know what he's doing and the pit of my stomach is rolling like a machine full of lottery balls.

"I'm so sorry, sir, please don't punish me. I'll watch my tongue in future, I promise."

"You will do wench, but you still need punishing. Stand up."

I jump up off the sofa like I bounced up on a broken spring.

"Now young lady, follow me." He stands up and walks me back out into the corridor then across it to a room I've not been in before. One of many actually from the length of the corridor and the doors along it. When the door swings open, I can see clearly that it's a study.

An old wood desk dominates the middle of the room. It's back faces a massive window which shines as black as Whitby jet filled with the night sky. In one corner of the room is a simple high backed chair with no arms. This is where he chooses to sit down and after shutting the door behind me I stand before him.

"Now only a young, foolish child would speak without thinking, so you'll receive a childish punishment. Over my knees now young lady." I hesitate, biting my lip. "NOW!" He barks, making me jump. "Don't question me young lady, or you'll not be able to sit down for a fortnight."

I concede and lower myself awkwardly to his lap, the bottom of my clothed breasts rubbing the outside of his thigh, my pubis pushing gently against the other. He quickly raises my skirt, folding it back over my bottom then he rips down the satin black knickers beneath.

He rubs his hand gently over the curve of my buttocks and I bite my lip, not wanting to moan out in case it enflames him more. I've never been spanked before but my cunt is wet and my nipples aching. However I'm not sure how much pain I can take. The idea is pleasurable, but the practicalities of it all make me anxious. I want to enjoy it, it's obviously something he enjoys; I can feel his erection against my stomach. But I just don't know how much punishment I'll be able to take.

Suddenly, the thought is shocked from my mind as his usually soft hand slaps down with stinging harshness. It shocks me but it isn't too uncomfortable. The next slap creates more heat than sharpness. I gasp and press my pubis forward trying to escape the next slap. It burns and I really start to question how much I can take.

It's then that he gently caresses my burning rump and I mewl like a contented kitty until he snaps his hand back and slams it against my flesh several times in quick succession making me yelp with the stinging pain.

His fingers skim over my heated flesh then dip between my buttocks, tracing down between my thighs as they fall open for him, dipping into the moisture pooling there and gently teasing my clit.

"Such a horny little slut, enjoying her spanking." He tuts and slaps my buttocks hard once more. I feel tears testing the corners of my eyes and want to yell out for him stop but I hold it in while the next two slaps fall.

"Stand up, wench." He commands and I comply, though my legs feel shaky, and my knickers are dangling between my knees, making it decidedly difficult to stand up and keep my balance at the same time. He grabs my arm and drags me; well he never gets far in front of me so it's more like he's roughly leading me actually, until we reach the hefty desk. He kisses me and whispers in my ear. "You're so fucking sexy, damn it." He presses me down against the cold hard wood until my cheek is lying flat against its shocking coldness and my breasts are pressed down hard against the surface.

"Spread your legs," he commands and I stretch them as far as I can, which actually isn't far with the knickers hobbling me. Mike flips up my skirt exposing my still stinging buttocks to the air and his eyes. His soft lips kiss the reddened flesh evoking a gasp at the tenderness in the action. I close my eyes and wait for what will come next. I hear the clink of a belt buckle, and hear him curse as he struggles to undo his zip. I wonder if he's having problems getting his hard on out. I could feel its stirrings pressing against my stomach when he spanked me, and I know it's a solid robust thing, not made for bending or getting out of tight places. Getting into them; well that's a whole different issue. The tell-tale crinkle of a condom packet heightens my anticipation. I know he's going to fuck me and I can't wait.

Gently he guides his erection inwards and downwards in a sweeping movement. He glides into me, my natural lubrication easing his way. I really am a slut to be so turned on from just a spanking. I grasp onto the table edge as he powers into me. He's crushing me against the wood but I don't care because his cock is caressing all my sensitive spots in this position. I'm shaking and spasming with a chain of orgasms within the matter of a few strokes.

"Fuck me, sir. Fuck my slutty cunt sir, please sir."

"Oh, fuck yes, I will." He curses, his fingers digging in to my hips, his cock slamming into me with such force that I feel the desk rattle below me, echoing the shudders that run through my body. Harder he forces into me, my body aching and tingling with pleasure. The hot flesh on my arse responds to every slap of his pubis against it.

"Oh fuck. I'm going to come, wench." He groans and I feel him withdraw.

The condom snaps off and I hold my breath. He wasn't planning to fuck me bare back surely? I'd have to use my safe word before he did that. I strained my hearing to get a clue of what would happen next and I heard his hand running up and down his dick. He was masturbating and I relaxed. He wanted to come over my arse. That I condoned, liked in fact. I was eager to feel his mark upon me. He shouts out his orgasm and the thick, warm liquid coats my butt cheeks. A shudder of residual sexual pleasure runs through me. I feel like I am now stamped as his possession.

"Well, I hope you'll be a good girl in future," he lectures as I straighten up.

"Of course, sir." I wink and after a moment of his stern look he chortles and I join in with the joyful laughter. Once I'm dressed I walk with Mike to the kitchen and perch on the light wooden stool by the breakfast bar while he prepares dinner.

"Pizza or Indian?" He asks.

"Pizza." I reply, nodding.

"Flavour?"

"I'm a pepperoni girl myself."

"Pepperoni it is then, I'm not fussy." he dials the number on the leaflet, orders two large pizza and puts the phone down.

"Do you ever cook in here?"

"Occasionally." He replies solemnly, "But Mary, my cleaner, prefers it if I don't."

We laugh, and he disappears into one of the myriad cupboards surrounding us. The kitchen is bigger than my whole flat put together. He returns with a bottle of red wine and two sparkling glasses.

"Ok, we're all set. Let's go to the living room and wait for the pizza. We can watch a movie whilst we eat it if you like."

"Sounds good to me," I reply and I love the domesticity of this scene compared to the kinkiness we'd experienced. This is what was missing from my relationship with Nick. I follow him back down the corridor and into the living room. He switches on a lamp as we walk in. He then walks round the room, lighting candles.

"I know, it's archaic, but I do prefer the candle light, it's so much softer, looks better in this house."

"I love candle light," I answer. "It hides all my flaws."

"What flaws?" He questions.

"Oh, you know, you've seen my wobbly stomach and that birthmark on my hip."

"I've seen them yes," he replies sitting down beside me and stroking my stomach, "but I've only admired their beauty. You're gorgeous all over, Caitlyn."

I don't know how to respond to that so I just smile. I've never had a man be so reassuring and confident before. In the past if I got emotional my boyfriends freaked out.

I don't pay much attention to the images on the screen while we wait for and then eat our pizza, washed down with the soft and rich red wine. As has been often the case of late, my mind is full and I'm plagued by questions and wonderings.

"I've never been spanked before." the words leap from my mouth as I think them.

"Never?" he asks, turning away from the TV screen to face me.

"No, never." I reply, not sure what to add.

"You did really well then, it was a total turn on for me, did you enjoy it?"

"Oh yes." I reply, "Yes, I did, a lot."

And that was the problem really, I enjoyed it a lot, and I wasn't sure what that meant.

"What's up?" he asks, putting an arm around me, I move away from him, so his hand just brushes down my arm.

"I don't know." I snap, frustrated now. "I don't know, this is just all very, surprising."

136

He nods, resting his hand on my thigh.

"I've always been in control Mike. I pick who I go out with, who I fuck - to put it at it's crudest level - and I was always in charge, totally in control." I turn my body to face him more, needing him to understand, for some unknown reason needing to reach out to him, to let him know how I feel. This is a completely foreign sensation in itself.

"And here, in this, well, relationship." Oh God, I said the R word, but he doesn't look like he's about to run off, "I've not been in control for a moment. I've been constantly surprised and taken off guard and lead. I've been lead. And it, it well, scares me Mike. It scares me that I trust you so much. I don't do trust, I just don't and now suddenly I am and I just don't..."

Tears fall completely unbidden, they just happen, and I can't hide them as when I try I end up sobbing and blubbering in a very unladylike way.

"Oh, Caitlyn." He shuffles closer and wraps his arms around me. "It's okay, it's okay."

He pulls me into his body, and I am enveloped by his heat and warm citrus smell. I press my face into his shoulder and I try and force my tears to stop, but the damn things keep on coming even with my eyelids closed.

"Oh Caitlyn, there's no need to be scared, love. No, you're as in control of all this as I am. Just one word, one word and I'd stop. Anything at any point. I'd never, ever force you into something, Caitlyn." He must anticipate my rejoinder as he carries on with barely a pause. "I know, I know when you first discovered who I was, that I was forceful, I know. But I could see in your eyes you wanted to, I just needed to break through the mental barrier. I'm so sorry, my damn manly impatience made me do it in such a harsh and stupid way. I'm so sorry, I don't ever want to hurt you or upset you at all."

His words soothe me, I can feel the genuine emotion behind them and I push myself out from his body to look into his eyes.

"It's not your fault." I sniff, finally halting the annoying tears. "It's my damn screwed up life. I guess, well, I guess I'll get used to this." I look up into his soft stare. "Will I?"

"If I have anything to do with it you will." He laughs and I see the affection dancing in his eyes so I laugh too, the anxiety rolling away as our lips meet in a soft, caring caress.

"Sorry about all that, I don't know what happened there, I'm not a crier." I sniffle then take a sip of my wine.

"Oh don't worry about it, emotions are slippery things and tears are nothing to be embarrassed by." He gently squeezes my hands. "So feel free to cry on me whenever you feel the need, all right?"

"Oh, you better hope you've not just discovered my inner cry baby then, or I'll soak that shirt right through at that invitation."

We both laugh heartily, needing to lighten up after that moment of intense sharing. Emotions, sharing, tears... I've never had this in a relationship before. Maybe I'd never been in a proper relationship before? Now there's a revelation.

"Well actually, I was planning to take my shirt off, using the excuse that your tears had soaked it through." He unbuttons the expensive dark material.

"Oh that's more than fine by me, as long as I'm allowed to kiss all the exposed flesh. Just to kiss and make up, you know."

"All the exposed flesh?" Mike grins wickedly, pausing with the last button half released.

"Yep, all of it."

"Oh well in that case..." He stands up and whips off his pants and boxers.

"Here you go, knock yourself out!"

I stand up and kiss him. Slowly I feel our lips throb and ebb together, my hands wrap around him and stroke down from the bottom of his hair to his broad shoulders. His hands clasp my waist and gently rub over the curve of my hips. I break the kiss and trail across his cheek and down the side of his neck, nibbling in combination with kissing. I feel his fingers clenching in response.

Lower my lips skim over his collar bone. My hands cup the end of his thick shoulder blades, roam down his arms as I kiss his chest, nipping and nibbling at each nipple, enjoying the strong, masculine skin beneath my lips and between my teeth.

I feel his knees trembling and taking pity on him I lead him over to the sofa. I make him lie down on his stomach. I want to tease him and don't want to be distracted by his fine erection and my need to feel it deep in my throat. I'll do that later.

Much later, I'm going to enjoy this. I want to show him that I do care, that I'm in this for more than the short term mind blowing sex. I guess I have my doubts, but he's got to have his too. I used Nick, or so it seems and this guy is in a top prestigious job. A scandal could ruin him. He has a lot invested in this relationship, and I want him to know that so do I, that he can trust me because I trust him.

I kiss over his shoulders, my hands smoothing over the skin of his lower back, my lips tickling lower as I nip at the side of his ribcage, making him chuckle. I continue to the small of his back and kiss the cute dint there. My tongue lazily circles around the area then I dip down between his firm buttocks and dart my kisses back out moments later.

I enjoy the hiss and moan of his breathing as I gently kiss each buttock. I caress the soft, peachy skin with my plump lips. I skim down to the join of his bum and his legs, down over his thigh and I tickle him again with the heavy pressure of my mouth on the back of his knees.

"Turn over." I ask and he responds. I bite my lip when his arousal becomes more than obvious, towering from his crotch. My body buzzes with anticipation and the sensitive skin itches with joy every time I move in my clothing.

An idea forming, I stand up and grasping the bottom of my top I pull it up and over my head. Next comes the black satin bra, and I can feel his eyes on me as my breasts slip out into the warm, wood smoke scented air. Slipping off my skirt takes just a moment and the knickers are removed just as simply. I once again sink to my knees at the bottom of the sofa, and begin by taking his left big toe into my mouth.

Feet are not intrinsically sexy in my mind, but the mock fellatio I practice on Mike's precious piggies arouses me to such a point that I slip a hand between my thighs and gently stroke up and down my slit. When both feet have been teased I slip up over his ankles and along the outside of his thigh.

Skirting around his crotch I kiss up the side of his ribs because I love the way he giggles when I do and over onto his stomach. I tease his belly button dip with the tip of my tongue then move higher to nibble and lick at his nipples. A brief kiss on his lips starts my journey back down again and while I taste his nipples once more, I feel his hand cupping my buttock.

He squeezes my flesh and my lips linger, then kiss lower. Right down to the tips of his toes I go again, pulling my bum reluctantly away from his touch to start my journey up the inside of his legs. Climbing onto the sofa between his spread legs I lick and nibble my way up to his soft, tender thigh flesh and higher 'til my lips kiss his straining, scrunched up scrotum.

"Oh, yes," he hisses, when my lips finally contact his genitals, my tongue lapping up to tease the very base of his straining cock. My hands cupping his hips, my body pressed flat against the sofa, my legs from the knees down hanging in fresh air. I keep my knees bent, my ankles linked and my legs bobbing slightly up and down.

My kisses trail up the underside of him, from the base to the top most tip. I lick out and taste the liquid pooling there. A sweet, bitter essence that I enjoy as I place my lips around him but barely touch him. I move my lips down just past the top of his head. I slither my tongue out and wipe it around him, like I'm licking up the drips from a whippy ice cream in summer.

He moans desperately and I can no longer continue to tease him, I need to taste him properly. I swallow his erection. With every subsequent sweep down I move lower, and lower, pushing more of him into my throat, testing my reflexes and the stretch of my lips till I manage to swallow his whole length.

"Oh, fuck!" He moans between clenched lips, thrusting up into my mouth. I feel him throb and twitch and the longing to feel his dick between my thighs becomes too much. Removing my lips from his cock, I stand up.

I find my handbag resting on the side table and pull out a condom.

"Oh, hurry," he begs, "please hurry."

I nod and place the condom between my lips. I walk back over to the sofa my mouth stretched with the latex sheath I kneel and run it down over his straining erection. As soon as he's properly wrapped I jump to my feet then throw my thigh over him. I move myself into position, my thighs outside of his, his cock nudging my hole.

He reaches between us and grabbing his hardened rod he pushes it inside my wet hole. Lavishing him with affection has aroused me almost as much as it aroused Mike. He slips in without any trouble. I'm soaking wet. I love mouth-fucking a guy. Fucking him properly beats it though and I rise and fall slowly on Mike's dick, enjoying every quiver that's sent through my body.

It's funny that right now, after a talk about control and not being in control, I end up on top. I measure the pace, pressure and length of the stroke, and have the power to satisfy or to tease. I try to move in a way that gives us both the greatest pleasure. He snakes his fingers between our bodies, seeking out my clit and I smile at his thoughtfulness then gasp when the pleasure pressure builds higher with every flick of his fingertips.

I look down on him and find his gaze is fixed on me. His dark eyes are lightened with liquid lust, his cheeks flushed, his hair matted and disorganized. I can see the impending orgasm in his eyes, his lips curl slightly and I smile in response. We keep eye contact as we fuck. However, I have to close my eyes when the shockwaves through my cunt are just becoming far too much, the intensity causing me to throw back my head and moan.

I bounce and gasp. I feel everything tighten and clench up in preparation for the onslaught of orgasm, then it all unwinds and

I straighten and shudder, yelling out his name. Just a moment after I yell I feel his cock shudder inside of me and hear him roar his completion.

"Oh hell, Caitlyn, you blow me away." He gasps and I collapse to his chest. He wraps me in his strong arms.

"You're pretty damn spectacular yourself, mister." I reply, nuzzling happily into his neck, enjoying the feel of his heat surrounding me, pacified by the beat of his heart.

Chapter 22

I seem to spend more time thinking about Mike now than thinking about anything else. It's worrying. I smile and sigh when I hear love songs. I keep thinking I see Mike in the street and I can't eat or sleep. He's constantly in my mind and well, everyone knows what that means.

However I can barely think it to myself, so I can't be, you know, falling in love - can I?

I guess I don't really know. I've been in lust a lot, I've had my fair share of crushes and a scattering of obsessions, but when I think back, I've never been in love. Yeah, I've said it, I've said it to a few long term boyfriends, but I don't think I ever meant it, I never believed it myself.

I suppose that the fact I'm even contemplating it being love this time might actually point to it really being love. If so, I'm not sure I'm wholly enjoying it. I don't know whether I'm coming or going most of the time, I feel out of control and that's uncomfortable for me.

I think the positives might just outweigh it though, I find myself smiling a lot. I'm just happy all the time. I feel cherished and special and the sex is absolutely, fucking amazing. What more could I want.

It's a long time since I've felt joy like this. It's just that it's the knowledge that this may be love on my behalf that brings up so many questions. Like how does he feel about me? What happens if he does love me, or what happens if he doesn't? Should I tell him and if so how and when? Or should I wait for him to say it first?

I am sick of being plagued by so many questions! Maybe I need to confront this thing head on, no use pussy-footing around. I should ring him up, invite him for dinner, then woo him with my beautiful home cooked food by candlelight. Well, I'll put the trays in the microwave, that counts as home cooked, right? Then I can tell him how I think I feel, and I can deal with what happens.

It might not be the perfect solution, but I can't carry on like this, I'll go grey by the end of the week. So I pick up the phone, and dial Mike's number.

"Hello." He answers, and his tone of voice seems different.

"Hi Mike, it's me, Caitlyn." I chirp, eager to make a date and get on with preparing for it.

"Well, you've got some nerve!"

"What?" My brows knit in confusion, and my smile disappears from my lips.

"Oh, don't even try the innocent routine missy; I know you're anything but."

"Mike, what are you on about?" Panic strikes into my heart now, on top of the confusion.

"Today's papers?" he asks, sarcasm dripping from his voice.

"What about it, I don't read them much anymore." I shake my head, wondering what's going on. He's not talking about the Nick incident again, because he said today's paper. Why would he be mad at me, for something in today's paper?

"Well I suggest you make an exception today." he says tersely then the phone line goes dead.

Sunday morning is not a time of day I associate much with, so I'm quite surprised by the number of people out and about on the high street, I even have to queue to pay for my newspaper. I didn't really need to buy it though. I can see what made Mike so angry splattered across the front page:

TV BOSS, KINKY SEX FIEND!

An anonymous source last night came to The Global News with a story of sexual debauchery. Who was it about? No, not one of the young impressionable stars of our day, but of Mike Masters, forty year old TV Chief.

Many of the photos were too explicit to publish but the few you can see really say it all. Kinky Mike is seen with a young girl over his lap, her buttocks exposed and red, his hand raised to place another blow.

"He likes his sex kinky." Our source tells us, the divorcee TV producer split from Ex-wife Germaine Hague three years ago, but no one ever knew why the split occurred. Now, on this revelation Germaine has revealed it was because she discovered her husband in bed with a girl, of barely legal age....

I can't read a word more, my eyes are glazed over with tears. He believes I wrote this, that I somehow took these pictures and I told the papers this, this awful pile of crap. I want to scream, I want to ring up the damn tabloid and tell them it's not like that: it's not kinky, it's not nasty, it's the most loving sex I've ever experienced in my life.

Not that it'd help, as the bastards would twist it to further back up their lewd tale of almost pedophilic sex acts. Maybe I should ring them and let them know the young girl involved is actually well over the age of consent. That in fact there's hardly any age gap at all.

Now, what can I do? How can I persuade him this wasn't me? All the 'evidence' points to it being me, but there's one flaw. How could I get a camera into a room I've never been in before?

Getting back to my flat, I look at the photos again. It looks to me like they've been taken from outside the window. They're dark and fuzzy since it was twilight when we fucked but there seems to be a glassy haze. The camera must have been outside looking in.

I've got to go and sort this out; I can't leave it like this. I might not have much to work with, but I've got to try.

Standing at his door, knocking for the tenth time, tears roll down my cheeks. I know he must be in, I can't imagine where else he could be. He's just ignoring me. How am I meant to clear my name, if he won't even let me in?

A light pings on in my brain and I hurry off towards the nearest supermarket, hopefully I didn't go through any speed cameras, because I know I broke the limit all the way there. I purchase a pen and a pad of paper, then buy myself a cup of tea and sit in the corner of the café, penning a letter, not quite a love letter, but one penned because I love this man.

I don't know how I'm so certain of it now, I just am, and I have to let him know, I can't let him go now. One page written, then discarded, another sentence written, another ball of scrunched up paper. Eventually, I write something I'm nigh on happy with, one last read before I post it through his door.

Dearest Mike,

I went and bought myself a paper, and was shocked at what I saw. I did realise why you were so short with me this morning though. But Mike, you have to believe me, those photos and that story are nothing to do with me. I swear on my life, on my mother's life, on the life of my stepmother's unborn child that I did NOT go to The Global News with all that crap, with those pictures.

I couldn't. Mike, this morning I rang you because I wanted to arrange a romantic dinner. I wanted to meet with you, to explain to you how strongly I feel about you, Mike; I wanted to tell you that I love you. I think I do anyway, I've never loved anyone before but I can't get you from my mind, I long to be with you every moment of every single day.

Please Mike, believe me, I'd never do anything to hurt you,

Please, please contact me soon,

Love,
Caitlyn x

I toy with putting in the things I suspect about the photo, that it's taken by someone outside and how could I plant a camera in a room, I'd never been in before in a house I barely knew the layout of? But giving excuses only seems to assume the party is guilty, trying to make a story to get out of it. No, he needs to work it out for himself. I just hope my letter helps, a bit at least, because, I can't bear to think of losing him. Tears slip down my face, and I wipe them away quickly, not wanting to show myself up in public.

I drive to his home and knock a few times, before sighing and slipping the folded piece of paper through the letter box. I drive home, sit on the sofa and turn the TV on.

I don't know what's on and I don't care. I just stare into the square box then I sob. I don't just cry, I sob. Great, loud un-ladylike noises spurt from my mouth and nose. My eyes stream with tears and my body shakes with the force of it.

I fall to my side and bury my face in my arm as desolate despair rips through my heart. Why? Why now? If I'd have not ditched Nick in it with the papers, this wouldn't be an issue now. This is my fault, all my fault.

I shouldn't have let Mike get to me like I did. I should have kept right on resisting that night, and left it as a mysterious encounter with a cowboy stranger. My heart wouldn't feel like it was about to burst right open if I'd left it at just one mind-blowingly awesome night of sex.

What have I got now? Several occasions of mind blowing sex and a damn broken heart. I was just working out I was in love, and what love was, and now it's pulled from me. That will teach me. It'll teach me to trust, to give something of myself. I'll not make love again, no. I'll keep to sex, just pure, seedy, lustful sex.

Nothing more, nothing deeper. No snuggling, no post orgasmic bliss.

My tears continue to flow like a waterfall. I've never cried like this before, not ever. So maybe that confirms this is love, was love. No. No, I won't believe it's over. Not until I have it written before me, or spoken in front of me. I just can't accept it being over; he'll come to his senses - won't he?

I must have fallen asleep on the sofa, as I wake up there, fully clothed, the TV blaring. I ring into work, I'm sick. I feel awful, my eyes are puffed up and my throat is dry from all the sobbing. I'm not going into work today. I just can't put myself through that. Not today.

Flicking through the TV channels, I tune in to the news, my jaw drops in shock as I see footage of Mike, shaking his head and pushing his hand into the view space of the camera.

"After allegations of paedophilic relationships with several girls, made in yesterday's Global News, TV chief Mike Masters has resigned. He has refused to speak out about the allegation, but his ex-wife, Germaine Hague, has openly spoken about the affair between the TV chief and a sixteen year old girl that brought their seven year marriage to an end."

"Bollocks!" I exclaim and fire a barrage of abuse at the petite, black haired harridan on the telly screen. I didn't imagine for a moment that Mike could be guilty of what she's accusing him off. In fact, I am pretty certain that I can smell a desperate publicity stunt when I see one. That woman wants money and fame.

I remembered then that she used to be kind of famous. Using my laptop I found out she starred in a couple of dramas and a second rate soap but all before her marriage and divorce from Mike. I was convinced she had completely fabricated the whole exposé just for her own gain. I recognize it because it's something I would have done. Fuck, it hurts to realise that you're the big bitch you've been accused of being for years. But then I suppose just knowing that could make me a better person. I take a deep, calming breath when tears jump to my eyes once again. Mike has made a big difference to the way I think. Being in love seems to have softened me, I've given myself permission to be involved with life again.

And I'll be buggered if I'm going to let some snotty actress ruin the best thing that's ever happened to me just to further her career. I'm not helpless in this situation. If I could scheme and scam my way into Nick's life how much more can I do to get back in with the man I love.

I have to switch off the emotions I was just getting used to playing with again to focus on my plan. I need to employ cold-hearted Caitlyn once more. It's harder than you might first think. Everything makes me think of Mike. Ordering in pizza, an old cowboy film on TV and my room, my haven just seems to be full of his scent and no matter how much of my perfume I spray I can't get rid of the citrus tang of him.

It takes a little while for my plan to come together what with all the distractions of a broken heart. I use the internet to find out all I can about Germaine Hague. It didn't take long as her career had been relatively short and not very illustrious. She lived off Mike while they were married and had obviously spent up her divorce settlement money and needed to make some more.

As I did more research it became clear that I needed to meet the woman in the flesh. But how? It wouldn't take me too much to find out her address, I know where to look and who to ask to find out such things. It's part of what makes me so good at my job. The problem would be getting her to speak to me. She obviously knows what I look like as she will have seen the sex tape in its entirety. So I will have to disguise myself. A bit of temporary hair dye, some fake glasses and a change of hair do and that's done. That's not a problem. But how do I get her to talk to me?

"Ms Hague? Hello, this is Tania Brightman from Hot Celebs Magazine."

I roll my eyes and her tone goes from frosty to excited in a matter of seconds. It's a good job I decided to do the initial meet over the phone.

"We would love to run an article on you in light of the recent scandal that your ex-husband has been caught out in. It must be heart-breaking for you."

"Oh, you wouldn't believe how much it hurts. It's brought it all back from when I found out about his dirty affair all those years ago, I can barely sleep I'm so upset by it all."

No wonder this woman needed help to get back in the lime-light, her acting is awful.

"Oh, I can't begin to imagine," I gasp, "we'd love to hear your heart-wrenching story and between you and me, I've been given a blank cheque to get the best, exclusive revelations from you. Can we meet up to discuss this in more depth?"

"If you bring that blank cheque with you, you can have whatever you like." Germaine giggles but I can hear the contentment of her greed in its timbre.

"Well, I am free later this afternoon. I have to be downtown for another story. Shall we meet at The Tea Rooms? I can get us a quiet booth if you'd like."

"Sure, shall we say 2 o'clock?"

"Yes, I look forward to meeting you then."

I slam down the phone after polite goodbyes and punch the air.

"Got you, bitch!" I yell and allow myself a slow smile of satisfaction. I will have the evidence to get Mike back by the end of day by hook or by crook. Fuck, I'll even sleep with the woman if I have to.

I arrive early at The Tea Rooms, plenty of time to chat with the owner who I know via work and who is eager to keep me happy. I'm surrounded by yummy treats and I have zero appetite. I am focused on the task in hand. I place my mobile phone on the table in front of me.

"Ms. Hague," I smile brightly and wave. I'd explained to Jane, the proprietor that I was using a different name. I told her I was a journalist on the side, she totally bought it. I really didn't want her getting involved too much though, just in case she lets my real name slip.

She smiles and glides over to my table, head in the air, expensive heels clacking on the wooden floor.

"Hi, Tania, I hope you've not been waiting too long." She shakes my hand and slides into the booth opposite me.

"Not long at all, really. Would you like some tea?" I gesture to the pot and cups in front of me.

"Oh, yes, please." She smiles, "I'm parched."

I pour the tea and leave her to add her own milk and sugar. I smile and press a button on my phone. "I'd better change this to silent." I explain, "I get so many calls and I don't want our meeting to be interrupted." She nods her ascent. I could almost see her ego inflating in step with her exaggerated self-worth.

"So, excuse me for being blunt," I say after a few lines of inconsequential platitudes, "but I'm here to get a story from you."

"Oh, yes, yes, certainly. What would you be after?"

"Well, I was talking to my editor and she really felt that the women of Britain really identify with your plight and want to know more about the story from your perspective."

Germaine nods like a dog in the back of an old car with no suspension.

"We're looking for something exclusive, shocking and personal."

"Like more detailed stills from the video? I have those. I can also give you more details about his affair, the age of the girl and

151

how that made me feel. But, it's my turn to be blunt, I need to know how much you'll pay me for these."

"Oh, I have been authorized to offer you this amount."

I push a cheque book towards her with an obscene amount of money written on it. "I'm afraid I can't go any higher, though."

Germaine attempted to look like she was seriously pondering if she'd take the deal or not. She looked like she was trying to get a stubborn bit of toffee out from between her teeth.

"Well, I suppose I can accept that, yes. The public needs to know what a bastard my ex-husband is."

I nod, smile and rip out the signed cheque. It's completely fake, but by the time she finds that out Tania will be long gone.

"So, where do you want to start?" I ask and Germaine pushes some photos across the table to me. I flick through them and try hard not to show any emotion on my face. I recall every photographed action in my mind, remember the loving touch of his hands on me and find the determination to carry on and clear my name.

"How did you come by these, they're so clear," I gasp.

"Well, just between you and me, off the record of course..."

"Yes, yes, of course." I smile.

"I got the old gardener's nephew to set it up for me. He's young, only twenty or so and he adores me. I told him I'd give him half the money I made and he bit my hand off."

"Really? Wow, very generous of you to give him all that money."

"Oh, I didn't give him a penny darling. He didn't deserve it. Stupid boy didn't even ask for any money up front."

"He deserves all he gets then, I say." I nod completely appalled by this woman's complete lack of morals. I listen half-heartedly as she makes up some pile of tosh about a young girl I'm sure she's made up. I pretend to take down notes in short hand. In truth I'm just scribbling. I want the vapid bitch to shut up so I can work out what to do next.

"I'll have to go Tania; I have an appointment with my agent after this. They're looking at getting me my own book deal, but that's hush-hush of course." She winks broadly. God, this woman is enough to make me feel sick.

"Oh, of course. I wish you all the very best," I really want to scream and shout and maybe gouge her eyeballs out for being such a nasty piece of work but I know I have to let her walk away. It's something far more important I have in my sights. I have to get Mike back.

I flick off the recording device on my phone when she leaves and rush home. I check the recording and you can clearly here that it is Germaine and what she's saying. I have evidence! I just now need the opening to offer it to Mike. I wash my hair until the temporary dye is washed away. I fling on some clothes that are more me and I walk over to Mike's house. There's a group of hungry looking journalists outside his gate so I keep walking round. I need to get in without anyone seeing me. An idea hits me as I recognize one of the vultures on my way past. I take my mobile from my pocket and dial a number.

"Hi, John, this is Caitlyn, hiya. I've just heard that Germaine Hughes is meeting her agent in Soho to secure a book deal. Great story in it if you get there quickly."

The minute he moves off with his cameraman the rest of the bunch follow. when they move off I move in and slip around the side of the wall. It's late afternoon on a Wednesday and its sheer luck that leads me to the gardener's boy.

He's raking up leaves into a huge pile. He is young, his hair close cropped and his jeans baggier than should ever be allowed but he is focused on his work and doesn't see me approach.

"Erm, excuse me?" I bat my eyelashes in my most seductive way.

"Oh, miss, I didn't see you there. You know you're not allowed in'ere, it's private property."

"I know, but I needed to have a word with you, what's your name?"

"Joel, Miss. I'm just here helping me old uncle. I'm not up to nothing bad."

"No, I know," I smile. The lad has misunderstood youth written in invisible ink across his forehead.

"It's just, Joel, I need you to do something for me. You see I just finished chatting to Germaine Hague."

"Oh, fuck!" He cursed, his eyes darted left and right as if looking for escape.

"Look, you're not in trouble, I promise. I just need you to back up my story. Germaine made you plant the cameras, right?"

"Yes, miss." He nodded, "I know it was stupid but she promised me a lot of money and well, my mum isn't well and the flat we're in is on the top floor and the lift breaks down so often. I just wanted to move her somewhere better and she offered me a shitload -excuse my French - of money, miss, I couldn't say no."

"I understand, Joel, I do. But you know she made up all that crap in the papers?"

He nodded.

"Well, all that crap made Mike, Mr. Masters, dump me. I'm his girlfriend, the girl in the video."

"Oh, miss, I'm so sorry, I shouldn't have done it but please don't tell the boss. He'll sack me and my uncle and then - please don't tell him, miss."

"My name is Caitlyn and I'm not going to tell him. I want you to tell him."

"What? You want me to tell the boss I invaded his privacy and dropped him in the shit?"

"Well, yes. But it'd help if you put it a bit more tactfully than that. Tell him Germaine tricked you into it. But whatever you do tell him it was her who employed you to take the video."

"Do you think I'm crazy? If I do that I'll be out on my arse quicker than me old man could say Jack fecking Robinson."

"I will make sure neither you nor your uncle get sacked, Joel. I promise. Mike is a good man and he'll realise that you didn't really mean any harm." I use my calmest tone of voice. I need to win this young guy over.

"She told me he was a pervert, I thought it was my civic duty to do something. I didn't want to make my money from a sex pest. But when I saw the vid," he had the decency to blush at this point, "I realised he was just having fun with a woman who was clearly of legal age. But the money miss, I mean Caitlyn, God, she offered me so much money."

"I know, Joel and that's what you need to explain to Mr. Masters. Can you do that for me?"

"I'm going to be sacked."

"Look, if you do get sacked I promise to find you a job. Hell, I'll pay you if I have to, I promise."

"Not good enough. I even got a fucking contract off Germaine and I've still got nothing."

"A contract?"

"Yeah, it's in me pocket. I carry it on me so me old mum doesn't find it. When she told me what to do and gave me the camera things I thought it best to have summat in writing, you know. In all them films and stuff they have to have a written contract. I thought I was being clever getting one." He fishes out a piece of paper, an old flyer but on the other side is a hastily scrawled contract with Germaine's signature at the bottom.

"You've got her signature, Joel. I'm sure Mr. Masters will believe you. It was clever of you to do that."

"Yeah?" he shrugs. "I'm not so sure."

"Look," I take out the notes I'd stuffed in my jacket pocket when I left. "I will give you all this and my assurances that if he sacks you that I'll take you on. Here's my business card. It's got my work and mobile number on it. Ring me. I'll make sure you get something good out of this, Joel, I promise."

"Oh, alright. I kinda trust you, bloody stupid of me really but there you go. And I do feel bad about doing that to Mr. Masters. He's been so good to me and my uncle. Plus you just gave me an 'undred quid. Money talks, miss."

"Joel, you won't regret this, I promise. Tell Mr. Masters that he needs to contact me, Caitlyn as soon as possible. I've got a taped confession of Germaine admitting to making you take the video."

"You have?"

"Yep."

"Why don't you just take that to him then?"

"Because he won't let me near him. He's pissed off. He thinks I shopped him to the papers. But if you tell him what happened he'll come to me, I know it."

"Alright, Caitlyn, I'll do it."

That short sentence gives me the most contentment I've felt in days.

Chapter 23

I'm not a spatient woman but I gave it time. I know Mike. He'll have to digest things before seeking me out. If Joel even told him anything. No, I mustn't doubt myself. I know characters and Joel would do the right thing I was sure. I just wish things would happen at my pace, life would be so much easier then.

Hell, I wish this whole misunderstanding had never happened, though then maybe I'd never have known just how much I love Mike. It's painful but I now know what I want. I want love. I've been convinced all my life that I didn't even need it. But I need love, I need Mike and it's as simple as that.

I am a nervous wreck. Work told me to take time off. Not a good sign I must admit but to be honest I couldn't concentrate if I was in the office anyway. I think the crying, wailing and indiscriminate sacking of anyone who came in to ask me what was wrong tipped them off and helped them figure out I was a little mentally unbalanced.

I have several weeks' vacation time stored up anyway. I'm a workaholic. Or I was. I never take time off, the firm often sends me off to far-flung corners, I can sightsee on the boss's dime. Good job I have the time stored up, I'd be out on my arse otherwise.

The phone rings. I grab it, wait a moment to calm myself then press the button.

"Hello?"

"Oh, hey baby, how're you?"

"Oh, it's you Dad. Yeah, I'm okay." I try to hold the disappointment from my voice.

"Good, baby, good."

"How's married bliss?"

"Hm, didn't you hear? We split up."

"Already?"

"Yeah, her parents didn't like me or you for some reason."

I smile wickedly then feel a pang of guilt.

"Sorry, Dad."

"It's alright; I don't think we were really meant for each other."

"You'll find the right one, Dad, someday."

"Well, maybe it's not meant to be, my love."

"You'll always have me, though." I choke up with emotion. Oh hell, what is wrong with me? I'm even being nice to my dad.

"I know, Caitlyn. I miss you, you know."

"We'll have to meet up, go out for a meal sometime."

"I'd like that," I hear the smile in his voice. "I have to go now, sugar but I'll call you when I'm next in the big smoke."

"I look forward to it." And you know what? I do. Life is too short to hold silly grudges and after all he is my dad.

"See you, babe."

I sniff, put down the phone and brush at my damp cheeks. I'm going completely soft. Bloody love. It changes everything about you. A sharp knock on the door makes me jump and I walk over dashing the tears from my cheeks. I don't even look up as I answer; convinced it's probably a salesperson.

"Caitlyn," The familiar voice has a gravely twang to it and his face is edged with stubble, his eyes are dark with lack of sleep.

"Mike, wow, I wasn't expecting you but come in, please come in." I babble on completely blown away by his appearance on my doorstep.

"I don't fucking know why I'm here, Caitlyn but I just had to see you."

"Sure, sure," I wave him past me into the flat. He's damp, his hair, his coat, and his jeans. I can smell the freshness of water on him but under it is a sharp hint of alcohol that worries me.

"Let me take your coat, would you like a drink?" I go into hostess overload as I click the door to and come to grips with the reality of Mike in my living room.

"I'm not here for a social call." He growls, "I want to know... something."

His brows knit and when he sways from side to side I realise he's more than a little tipsy.

"Okay, I'll tell you anything you want to know. I'll just go and make us some coffee while you're thinking."

"I don't want coffee." He snapped, "I don't want it at all."

I let him rant and prepare a pot of my favourite brew.

"Are you listening to me, Caitlyn?" He snaps and I look up.

"Yes, I'm listening. What do you want to ask me?"

"I'm still working on that." He mumbles and throws himself onto my sofa. I cringe as his wetness hits my suede suite. "But I'm not happy with you. Not happy at all. Oh, that's it!"

I pick up two cups and put one down on the table in front of him. I sit in the chair opposite and hold the cup close to my chest, savouring the bitter scent and the steamy warmth.

"Why the fuck did you talk to my gardener?"

"To find out the truth."

"To corroborate your version of the truth more like," he stabs a finger at me and it wobbles.

"Did you actually listen to what Joel had to say? Did you see the bloody contract?"

"You mean the bit of paper he'd forged my ex's signature on?" His words slur and I wonder how pissed he really is.

"You can honestly say you think I am more capable of selling out to the press than Germaine is? Really?"

"Yes," his wandering gaze alights on the cup on the table. He lifts it carefully with both hands and stretches out his neck to sip from it. He pulls a face then takes another sip.

"Well, thank you. Thank you very fucking much. I had the pleasure of meeting Germaine earlier this week and she is a sleazy fucking piece of work. She's a money-grabbing bitch of the highest order and Joel gives you her head on a fucking plate and yet you still think I dropped you in the dirt?" I take a deep, jagged breath. My heart contracts painfully. "I thought better of you. I thought we had something special as cliché as that is. I thought you were different."

"Oh, boo fucking hoo. I was just another notch on your post. Another fuck on your way to financial stability. I even bought that you didn't realise who I was. You missed your calling, you should have been an actress. I fell for it all. The cowboy and whore, the caring words, the fucking awesome sex. I thought, well, I thought that I could love you and then, well, then I read the newspaper and my whole world fell apart."

I sob and shake my head.

"I can't believe, I honestly can't believe you still think it was me. Could you ever trust me? If I had empirical proof to show you that I was innocent would that convince you or would you still doubt me? Am I that unimportant to you? Are you that convinced I'm evil?"

"It's just what you've proved to me, Caitlyn." He slams his cup down, hot liquid flies out all over the place but I don't care that it might stain. "Germaine was a money grabbing tart who fucked everything that she could get her hands on and finally I caught her out. I was watching you all the time, Caitlyn. Fuck, our introduction was rocky enough and what you did to Nick worried me. I found you out, girl, I found you out and it tore me apart."

"But could you ever trust me, Mike. Listen, I know you're drunk, I know you're angry but just think about this because what you answer will change how both our lives continue. Could you ever trust me?" I need to know. If he can't trust me then no matter how much I love him we simply can't be a couple.

He looks hard at me. I bite my lip and try to hold back the tears that prick and threaten to overwhelm me. I can see the thoughts flitting through his mind. His face crinkles with concentration. His breath comes in ragged gasps. He seems to be battling with something. I am scared to even breathe. His answer will change the course of my life, there's just no way I can deny it.

"I want to," he whispers, "I really want to."

"But can you?" I persist. "It's really important, Mike. I need to know."

"I think so." His gaze lifts to mine and I can see the uncertainty etched on his face but in the depth of his gaze I can see a core of something solid and dependable.

"Right, stay there. I have something to play for you." I go into my bedroom and pick up my phone. I walk back into the living room scrolling through to the item I want. I put it down on the table.

"Listen."

I press play.

And Germaine's voice comes through loud and clear. She'd not questioned my phone being on the table and so I picked up every nuance of her tone as she greedily accepted my offer to sell her ex down the river. I watch Mike. His eyes widen when he realises what he's hearing.

"Oh, fuck." He groans when I click off the recording. "Oh, shit."

He holds his head in his hands. "Fuck, fuck, fuck."

I don't know what's causing him to be so explosively expletive but I'm hoping it's because he's just found out he's been a complete bastard to me for the past few weeks.

"Oh, Caitlyn, I'm sorry." He looks up, "I'm really so very sorry."

I shrug, non-commitally.

"I've totally fucked up. I have. I knew, deep inside I knew you weren't like that. I knew it but I didn't believe myself. Shit. I'm so sorry, Caitlyn."

"You said that already," I sigh.

"Ooh, my head." He groans. "I don't feel too good, Caitlyn."

"No, I can see that. Come on, you need to lie down." I pull him up off the sofa. He leans heavily on me. I stagger a little under his unexpected weight. He is more inebriated than I thought.

"Will you forgive me?" he whispers, as if he's afraid of the answer.

"I want to," I reply, honestly, "but I'm not sure if I can yet. Let's sleep on it."

"Okay," he nods, "okay. I love you, you know that, right?"

"Well, you've never said it before."

"I do though, it's completely and absol-delinitely the right truth thing."

"I love you too," I maneuvered him toward the bedroom door. I am humouring him with my answer but I suspect the words said in jest are the closest to truth I will ever get.

"Good, Caitlyn, good."

I dump him on my bed. I pull off his jacket and his t-shirt. Both are wet. I go to get the washing up bowl to put down on his side of the bed then check that the door is locked and just gather my thoughts. All my cards have been played. I should be happy. Mike is in my bed. But he is drunk and all this may be forgotten in the morning. Really we're in limbo. There's no conclusion to my case and I'm just waiting for the judgment of the jury of one, Mike.

When I re-enter my room he's already under the duvet. I put the bowl down at his side of the bed along with a glass of water. I take off my clothes and slip on the first night dress that comes to hand then slide into bed next to Mike. His breathing is deep and even as I snuggle close. He's asleep. I let the rhythm of each breath lull me and roll away the stress of the day. I close my eyes and relax, safe in the knowledge that I will wake in the morning next to the man I love.

He's sleeping so soundly when I wake that I creep out from under the covers and leave him undisturbed. I feel this is all very surreal. I smile with the contentment of a good night's rest next to the man I love but yet at any moment he could wake and this perfection that exists while he sleeps could be shattered. I don't want that to happen but I need to find out for certain how he feels. My life is on hold until I know.

He said he loved me. I don't want that to turn out to be a lie just like it's always turned out to be before. It's been lust, it's been friendship, companionship, fetish even but never before has it ever been love. I decide I need to talk to him but instead of waking him up empty handed I brew a pot of coffee and cook a couple of slices of toast.

I'd make pancakes or create a deliciously greasy fry-up except for the fact I can't cook and I wouldn't know where to start. I carry the tea and toast through to the bedroom on a plastic tray.

"Mike." I sit on the edge of the bed and put the tray down on the side table. "Mike, love, I made you breakfast." I climb under the duvet and push my body up against his back. His only response is to push out his bum so he snuggles into the cup of my body.

I hook an arm over his waist and lean in to kiss the spot where his shoulders and neck meet. He murmurs but doesn't move. I pull myself closer to him. I am sure he can feel the tips of my hardened nipples through the thin layer of satin that lies between us. I keep kissing. I move along his shoulder and back again. I stroke my fingers through his wiry chest hair and wait for his reaction.

"Morning," he croaks, "oh, my head."

"Hey. Are you alright?"

"Well, I have the warmest, softest, sexiest woman in all the world snuggled against me in bed so I'm fucking amazing but I'm afraid some bastard is using a huge drill inside my brain and is making it really difficult to think, move or further appreciate the aforementioned hot woman who's lying next to me."

"Well, how about I get you something for the pounding in your brainbox then?"

"A big axe," he groans rolling over to face me. "Oh, remind me never to drink again."

"Yes, dear." I pat his chest, "I'll go and get you an aspirin."

"Caitlyn," I stop at his call and perch on the edge of the bed. "Yes?"

"I really would love to fuck you as soon as the drilling ceases and the world stops spinning."

"Sounds good to me," I reply, my lips bending easily up into a smile.

Moments later he's chugging down gulps of water and a little colour has returned to his cheeks.

"How much did you drink?" I ask. He lies back down very gently and very precisely.

"I don't remember but I picked up the alcohol when I first saw the papers and I haven't really stopped since."

"That explains a lot." I take the empty glass from his hand and put it down on the tray beside me. I nibble on a slice of toast and pass a piece to him. He pulls a face.

"You need to eat something or you'll just end up feeling worse." When had I become the sensible one? Now that's scary.

"Alright, alright, bossy."

We nibbled on cold toast in easy silence for a little while.

"Mike, where do we go from here?"

"Blimey, Caitlyn, lead me in to the day with an easy question why don't you?"

"It's been on my mind." I shrug.

"Me too," he confesses, "but the answer isn't a simple one because I don't really know it."

"Oh." I sound like a balloon deflating.

Mike turns to me, winces then kisses my cheek.

"But wherever it is, I'm going there with you, okay?"

I nod eagerly and tears of shock and joy tumble down my cheek. He gently rubs them away as they fall. I look up and can see the shimmer of tears in his eyes too. I close the gap between our mouths until we're kissing and all the fears, doubts and questions just melt away. It all becomes clear as the emotions we feel for each other freely flow between us. His love greets mine with an encompassing hug and soon enough our love is joined together and blended to a point where I don't know where to separate it. I don't want to.

Words are forgotten, his hands slip down onto my shoulders and I stretch out to keep the connection running. I stroke down his spine, enjoying the warmth of him against me. All the pain and second-guessing of our days apart melting away with each touch. I feel alive again.

I touch with a new awe. I'd been so close to losing him. I honestly thought I'd no longer have the pleasure of rubbing up against him. I'd never feel the comfort of his arms around me, the passion of his cock pressing into me. I had lost all hope of ever feeling fulfilled ever again. My heart swells with joy as he pushes my nightie up and over my hips. His hands possessively press against my flesh. I feel like he is branding me with his touch, that he's marking me as his.

I love it.

I want to feel his naked chest against mine so I lift away from him so I can pull off the silken barrier that separates us.

"Oh, yes," he murmurs when my naked breasts bounce into his view, "I have missed these beauties." He grabs and molds my tits eagerly and I giggle at his enthusiasm.

"Hey, what about me?" I playfully pout.

"Oh, yes, I missed you too," he clambers up onto his elbows with only a tiny wince at the protest of his hangover and kisses me. He balances on one hand and continues to squeeze from breast to breast with the other. "Hottest fucking threesome I ever want to enjoy."

"You've got this complimenting thing down pat haven't you?" I murmur between kisses.

"I'm not perfect yet; I will have to keep practicing on you possibly for many years to come." His kisses nuzzle my neck and I grip onto his shoulder for support. I'm dizzy with lust.

"I can learn to live with that," I mumble into his hair and run my fingers down his back. I love the heat of him beside me, I love his scent and the way the little patch of hair at the back of his head stands up when it's not been brushed into submission. I especially love the way his erection imprints its hard heat into my thigh as we embrace.

"I missed you so much, Caitlyn," He wraps his arms around me and pushes me down to the mattress. "It's so good to be with you again, to hold you."

"It's good to be held." I purr and spread my thighs to accommodate him.

"Oh, fuck, Caitlyn, I need you. I need you so fucking much."

I stroke his cheek and let the tear of joy slip from my eye while he watches.

"Take me," I whisper, the love I feel for him caught in my throat, making my words husky and deep.

"With pleasure." I nod towards the bedside table and he opens the drawer and withdraws a condom. Ripping the packet he sheaths his erection then pushes into me and I give around him like melted butter. I am so turned on that the barest brush of his pubis against mine electrifies me. I close my eyes, the sensations becoming too much. I need a shield to hold in everything that's washing over me. In the absence of said shield I just use my eyelids.

"Caitlyn," he murmurs, I wrap my legs around his waist and pull him tighter to me. "I love you."

My eyes flick open and I'm met by his intense stare. I smile.

"I love you, too." I'd always had huge problems with saying those simple words but with Mike they flew from my lips with surprising ease. He stretches forward, our lips meet and mimic the ebb and flow of his hips pumping. I am surrounded by him; I feel like I am blending into him and I don't want it to ever stop.

I want to come with him, I want to contract around his hardness so I slip my fingers down between our bodies, he lifts up to give me room.

"Yeah, come for me, Caitlyn, please. I want to feel you come."

It doesn't take much to push me over. I contract around him and he growls loudly. He holds himself inside me and collapses onto my chest. I wrap my arms around him. I run my fingers through his hair as we pant and gasp to get our breath back.

"Thank you," Mike murmurs.

"What for?"

"Not giving up on a stupid old idiot."

"Well, that idiot managed to embed himself in my heart so I couldn't do anything but." I reply.

"I'm glad. I was so miserable without you. I've just realised something incredibly profound."

"That I'm fucking awesome?" I smirk and he shakes his head against my chest.

"I knew that already," he responds. "No, I just realised that I'm nothing without you. That you're everything I need. You fulfill me."

"Funny that." I kiss his forehead. "I just realised the same thing."

Lightning Source UK Ltd.
Milton Keynes UK
UKOW05f0623111013

218839UK00001B/9/P